DAUGHTERS UNTO DEVILS

AMY LUKAVICS

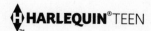
HARLEQUIN®TEEN

ISBN-13: 978-0-373-21158-6

Daughters unto Devils

Printed in U.S.A.

For my Edmund—
"A star shines on the hour of our meeting."

ONE

The first time I lay with the post boy was on a Sunday, and I broke three commandments to do it. *Honor thy father and thy mother, thou shalt not lie,* and *remember the Sabbath day and keep it holy.* Why couldn't I stop counting all of my sins? It was as if I was craving the wrath that was to follow them, *challenging* it, if only to make certain that I was, indeed, alive.

There used to be a time that I would have feared the consequences of acting out in such a way against the Lord, but not anymore, not after last winter, not after being trapped in the cabin for months and losing my mind and seeing the devil in the woods. Clearly, the Lord had forgotten all about me, and therefore I would no longer be following his rules.

"When I die, I will see Hell," I whispered after we were through with our sins of the flesh, but the post boy did not hear me over the sound of the water from the creek. "The devil has claimed me already."

I wished that the boy would turn over so I could study his face. I didn't know it very well yet, wasn't even sure if his eyes were brown or blue, to be honest, but I wanted that to change. This boy had saved me from my Hell on earth with the wonderful distraction that was his body. I should have known his name.

Henry, I remembered. *His name is Henry.* I asked him in a louder voice if he'd be coming back again to see me after today. He said he would.

"Good." I sighed and ran my finger slowly down his spine. "Because if you didn't, I would be cross with you."

He turned over then, not to kiss me like I hoped, but to contemplate me with genuine curiosity. His dark eyebrows furrowed. I noted that his eyes were green, like lucky clover, and that his nose was attractively askew.

"You're strange," he said after the silence became uncomfortable. "What's different about you?"

I was chilled at the question. *Too many things, Henry,* I thought. *This is only the second time we've ever met.* Still, the question awakened the memories of last winter unmercifully, the ones that were too painful to bear, the ones that ended up causing all sixteen years of my life to slip away from me like water through open fingers.

The screaming, oh, all that screaming, and the claws, and the bloody footprints in the snow, and the devil who knew my sins...

I noticed that Henry was still watching me in silence, waiting for my answer. *What's different about you, Amanda*

Verner? It would be a lie to claim that the question didn't irritate me; I was here for good feelings in abundance and good feelings only.

I pulled my frown into a shy grin. "I think I've already answered that question for you, have I not?"

"Oh, yes." He smiled, and kissed my fingertips. "I suppose that you have. The four-hour ride to get here was more than worth it, I would say. I hope you don't think less of me, pursuing your body with such haste—"

"Of course not." I cut him off with a kiss. "I know it is sinful, but it also feels...necessary. How can that be?"

And it was true. Already I found myself wanting to be with him again, my flame in the dark, my rescuer.

"I understand exactly what you mean." Henry's hand slid down my side, and I forgot all about the devil in the woods, as well as the secret that made him come for me in the first place. "I wonder how I went so long making deliveries to Crispin's Peak, never suspecting that the lady of my dreams lived right on the other side of the mountain."

I didn't like to imagine Henry leaving the mountain to deliver post to other settlements. The idea of not having a reason to steal away from the cabin and my family whenever the tension became unbearable was troubling, but Henry insisted that he wouldn't stay away long.

"I'll come back as often as my schedule allows it," he promised. "Worry not, sweetling."

After Henry's trousers were back on and he was riding away on his horse, General, toward the trail that would eventually lead back to the settlement, I walked home through the trees, pulling pine needles from my hair and securing the buttons at the neck of my dress with fumbling fingers. At the sight of the cabin I became overcome with a most indecent bloom of shame, the shame of sacrificing my body and liking it, *really* liking it. Did it mean I had no conscience? Pa would have certainly thought so.

Ever since I could remember he'd ingrained in us the knowledge that to betray our Lord was to betray ourselves, our *souls*. A woman's body was to be for her husband only, and anything less would result in the Lord's profound disappointment and, by extension, the dismissal of the daughter from the family. I wondered if Pa would really cast me out if he discovered what I had just done with Henry. Part of me believed he would, but it was hard to say.

I wished I could ask my sister Emily.

Emily is my dearest friend, after all. I do tell her *everything*.

But I haven't told her about Henry. She doesn't even know that he exists.

She doesn't even know that he exists and I've lain naked with him in the woods not once, not twice, but eight times now. And it's because of this that I think I must have truly lost my mind, because after witnessing the birth of my youngest sister, Hannah, I wouldn't wish pregnancy or child birth on even my worst enemy.

Hannah.

On more occasions than I care to admit, my mind creeps to a dark, spider-webbed place where my new baby sister is the reason I've turned into such a soulless liar.

Because sometimes in the blackest depths of the night, I pray for something bad to happen to Hannah. Sickness maybe, or a quick accident during her bath. The horrible thoughts pain me, cause me to sob quietly into my pillow, but I become temporarily numbed from the evil as I think about my ma and how much she has changed since the winter and the sickness and the birth.

How much we all have.

The woman who wove grass halos for Emily and me when we were children is long gone, a slave to the unconditional love she has for her poor, helpless baby, born deaf and blind and full of confused rage as a result of it all. Ma's worry for Hannah never ceases, never slows, constantly showing itself through dark circles under her eyes and a newly formed hunch in her stature that wasn't there before last winter.

(Could it be I who is responsible for those circles? I who have pulled her shoulders down with the weight of the entire world? I cannot bear the thought, no, it must be the baby, the ever-wailing baby who screams with such tremendous, earned rage.)

Surely if the baby hadn't survived the birth, things wouldn't be as dire as they are now, as positively *changed*. So I bring myself to pray for Hannah's death, *beg* really, and am afterward reduced to a shriveling shell of a girl with no soul and a craving for the odd post boy who likes having his parts tugged.

Of course, after the tears dry up and I'm left hiccupping in bed, I realize that what I'm doing is despicable and morbid and wrong. The Lord would hate me for wishing death upon one of his creations, but by now I am quite certain that the Lord hates me anyway.

Sinner. My wish for Hannah is my darkest secret, the one that called the devil upon me, the one that will be my undoing.

When I remember this the tears usually start again, this time rolling down a face that burns with regret and shame. Shame, the constant. Shame, the stain on my soul that can never be washed away.

I heard once that long-term isolation can have an effect most wicked on even the most competent of minds and seasoned mountain men, and also that guilt on its own is capable of ruin. By the time I met Henry the post boy in Crispin's Peak while I was in for supplies with my pa, I'd experienced both, and my mind was eaten with rot.

I believe a part of myself may have died last winter.

TWO

Sometimes I believe the baby will never stop crying. How scared she must be, or angry, or both. Ma often wonders aloud if it's possible she's in any sort of pain, cursing the absence of a real doctor on the mountain. Pa gets upset if anyone makes such remarks in front of him, and tells us that it's a sign of an unsympathetic heart. Emily watches from the outside, observant as always, a frown painting her face with unease at the sight of our parents quarreling.

After Hannah finally quiets down for the night and the cabin is saturated in shadow, Emily gets up in th dark from the goose-feather mattress on the fl we share with our younger siblings Joanna She walks on soft toes to my side of th in next to me without a word, the to make sure she hasn't awakened a ing in a hushed whisper if everything

"Why must you keep asking me that?" I whisper louder than I should, exhaling my irritation.

"You've been so quiet lately," she insists. Pa's snores cut through the cramped blackness of the cabin. "I know that something is happening in your head. Why won't you tell me?"

I want to, more than anything, but I cannot. I can hardly even admit what I've done to *myself*, even though my bleeding cycle has been missed many times, and my breasts ache like never before, and I feel horribly nauseous every single morning and sometimes late at night, just like Ma was when she first suspected she was with child with all of my siblings.

It shouldn't have come to this, but there is no way to avoid it. Not after the secret get-togethers in the woods behind my family's cabin, not after the hidden flowers and candies started showing up in the bushes by our meeting place, not after the kisses where Henry's tongue was in my mouth and his hands were pressing my body against his, like if he didn't have me soon he'd absolutely *die*.

Desire rules all, for better or for worse. I was doomed from day one.

And now *I'm* to be a mother, when I do not even be-
eve that having children is smart or favorable or lovely.
re mouths to feed, more people to keep alive, more
es for disease and pain and grief. In the end, it

is hard to think that it could ever be worth it, all those years, all that unnecessary pain.

I search for Emily's eyes through the dark.

"Everything is well, sister," I lie.

After her frustrated sigh causes Ma to stir, my sister reluctantly turns over and falls asleep against her better judgment, I'm sure. Soon she is snoring softly, completely unaware that I am biting the corner of my pillow and curling my toes into the bottoms of my feet to keep from screaming.

Secret is not something that belongs in Emily's or my vocabulary. Then again, neither is anything about lying, or being with child at sixteen years old when I have no husband to claim the infant as his. I promised after last winter that I would never lie to her again, and here I am, betraying her trust. When she finds out about the baby, the brittle bone of that trust will shatter, impossible to fix, impossible to reverse.

Besides Emily, I also have the reactions of my parents to fear. Ma will weep, undoubtedly, too overcome with disappointment to function. Pa will call me a whore, he'll call me a sinner, he'll throw me out on my own as proof that my misgivings will not bring down his own faith. One bad apple could spoil the entire barrel. Unsympathetic hearts, indeed.

I might as well be dead.

But...what if I run away with Henry and they never have to find out? My toes curl in the dark even harder.

If I disappear, my family would probably assume that I was attacked by one of the many bears or wolves that roam the mountainside where our cabin sits, that I was ripped up and fed to a pack of hungry cubs in the name of the Lord.

They would be taken with sorrow over the loss, yes, but they would move forward eventually, especially knowing that I was with our Heavenly Father and waiting for them to join me. They'd never know the truth, not until they died and ascended into their eternal kingdom and noticed that I was still missing.

I must take control of my fate. Tomorrow is the first of the new month, and Henry will surely show up for a secret visit. So tomorrow, I will tell Henry about the baby. If he really loves me, as he's claimed breathlessly over and again during our nude entanglements in the forest, he should be happy. Maybe even more encouraged to bring me home with him this time.

With the resolution bound in my mind, I begin to cry into the pillow that I am still biting on as if my life depends on it. I will never see my dearest friend again. I imagine Emily alone with Joanna and Charles and Hannah. I imagine her taking a walk through the misty woods after finding out that I have gone missing, just so that she can cry and curse privately over her loss, and my heart aches unbearably.

This is when I identify the part of my resolution that I could never follow through with, and I adjust the plan accordingly by swearing to myself that I will come back for Emily, after the baby is born and I am married and can offer her someplace to live, along with a proper explanation of why exactly I had to do this.

I had to go away, I imagine myself telling her in the future. *You know why.*

And that is how I make myself comfortable with it, that is how I stop the tears and cool my face of its shame and uncertainty. I stop biting my pillow and lie on my back and fall asleep to the sound of Pa's serrated snores for what may very well be the last time. Emily sighs beside me and pushes her ice-cold feet against my calves to warm them.

I will miss her so much.

I dream about darkness and punishment and something that is squirming inside of me, writhing, growing bigger and stronger with every cursed, miserable heartbeat.

Emily asks me what's wrong again the next morning, this time with more urgency.

"You *know* I'll find out eventually," she challenges with a forced smile. "I am your sister. It's part of me to know when something is wrong with you."

She molds small discs of cornmeal batter with her hands and places the cakes on the large skillet that is already sizzling with strips of boar bacon, still fresh from Pa's catch yesterday evening. The fragrance of the breakfast and the black coffee bubbling over the fire just outside the cabin is wonderful in the early morning of these woods, before the baby is awake and screaming and reacting violently to anybody who attempts to touch her except for Ma. A family of deer graze around the trees nearby, slurping up the cold, dew-soaked grass that blankets most of the mountainside.

I turn the hot, spitting meat strips with caution while I try to think of what to say to Emily.

"If you'll find out eventually," I tease, no longer able to keep up with the *nothing*s, "then I might as well wait until you do."

"Oh, please!" Emily pinches me playfully on the elbow. "Just skip to it."

Emily deserves everything and more for still treating me like me, no matter what, even after I broke down to her about the truth of what happened to me in the cabin when Hannah was born. She promised to take my secret to the grave, but still I found that everybody else in the family was different around me once the winter was gone; they were hesitant, cautious, almost as if they were *afraid*. Joanna and Charles started to prefer Emily to oversee their games instead of me, although I suppose I couldn't blame them for it.

I would be afraid of me, too.

"It's nothing, sister," I insist, willing her to just believe me and move on from it. "Truly."

A wave of nausea overcomes me, and suddenly the

smell of the food is too much to bear. I place my sleeve over my face and feign a cough so that Emily thinks it's just the smoke from the fire.

"You're acting very curiously," she observes as I take small gulps of the fresh morning air to fight the roiling in my gut. "You almost look ill, or something."

"I am just fine." It comes out with far more bite than I intend. "You do not need to worry about me, Emily." I manage not to wretch up any bile, and before I know it the moment of sickness has passed. I load a plate for Pa and try to ignore how my sister watches me from the corner of my eye.

"Joanna and Charles asked me to take them into the forest while Hannah naps," she says, and clearly this means she has given up on pestering me for now, for which I am relieved. "I'd ask you to come along, but something tells me that this is going to be one of those days where you disappear into the woods for hours."

She is frowning as she speaks. In the past when I've met up with Henry, I'd tell Emily that I felt like taking a long private walk to gather my wits and enjoy the silence away from the baby. From the beginning she insisted that she understood and never questioned me about it, her own way of proving that she was ready to forget about the past, I suppose.

I think about how Emily's face looked when I promised that I wouldn't hide things from her anymore. *You are* sure *you're going to be all right, Amanda?* she had said with tears in her eyes after I'd finished telling her about the devil in the woods. *You're certain?*

Yes, I had replied, about a week or so before I went on the supply run to the settlement with Pa on a whim and met Henry for the first time. *I swear it, sister.*

The thought saddens me so much that I seriously consider telling her about the baby for just a second. I refrain, of course. Emily carelessly tosses pieces of cornmeal cake and meat strips over the various plates, then pours some coffee for Ma.

"I still think you're hiding something," she grumbles and makes her way to the front door of the cabin, plates of breakfast carefully lined over her forearms. I grab the last two plates and follow after her, my breath caught in my chest.

Ma shuts the cabin door behind me, as softly as possible, and motions for me to keep my feet light as she nods to my baby sister. Hannah is still sprawled motionless on Ma and Pa's bed, but any excess vibrations could wake her in an instant. Ma takes the plates from me and nods her thanks, just as I realize what's about to happen. Sadly, the warning does not come soon enough.

The burning vomit sprays from my mouth and nose before I even have a chance to turn, splattering over the plates and Ma's arms and the wooden floor of the cabin. I cry out in horror and turn to push the door back open.

"Amanda!" Ma nearly drops the plates as she follows

me to the well outside. She peels the wet stinking sleeves of her dress down her arms. "Are you falling ill, my dear? It's been too long for it to be the sickness from last winter." The last bit ends up sounding more like a paranoid confirmation to herself, and I feel wretched for stirring up the memory.

We get to the rain barrel, and I splash my face with the cold water. I swish some of it around in my mouth and spit into the bushes while Ma washes her arms.

"I'm so sorry, Ma," I finally manage after I've finished. I take a few sips of the water and it tastes terrible, sour and rancid. "Maybe I am. I feel well enough now, though. And I'm not feverish, so please do not worry. I will be fine."

The sound of Hannah's off-key screams and yelps begin to pour from the open cabin door. Pa calls for Ma impatiently from inside. Emily emerges from the doorway with a clean dress on her arm for Ma and a rag for me. Ma dresses quickly as Hannah's cries escalate, and the circles beneath her eyes look even darker than usual. She refuses to go back inside until I assure her three more times that I feel all right.

"What is happening?" Emily asks me after Ma has retreated into the cabin. I take the rag from her and wipe my face, as well as the back of my neck.

"The breakfast plates," I say instead of answering. "Is there still enough food to go around? I don't have to eat. And Joanna and Charles—"

"—can share a plate without raising a concern." Emily cuts me off impatiently. "But forget about the food. Sister, you're ill!"

"You just heard me say that I feel much better now," I insist and take her hand. "Let it pass. I really don't believe it's anything to get concerned about."

"Your *behavior* is what's to get concerned about," Emily snaps. "You said you wouldn't hide things from me anymore." She crosses her arms over her chest.

I've been sleeping with a boy you've never met, over and over, and you never even became suspicious about it. No matter how hard I try to say it, my lips remain closed.

"Amanda," Emily says again and steps closer. "You can tell me. Did it happen again? Are you starting to—"

"It's *nothing*, I said!"

Hannah's cries finally cease. The difference in sound is startling, and I take the opportunity to leave my sister behind so she won't have the chance to break me down.

"Amanda," Emily calls after me, but I keep walking. Pa is about to depart, to hunt some furs to sell. He doesn't ask me if I'm all right.

The vomit-speckled plates are piled in the dirt next to the water trough just outside the cabin. Tiny winged bugs crawl over the shiny slime that coats the cornmeal cakes, and I plead with God in my head to let the water in my stomach stay down.

When I enter the cabin, Ma is with Hannah on the rocking chair that Pa built for her as a wedding present. Everyone has finished eating already, and there is half a plate waiting for me. The smell of the meat is too atrocious for me to even consider it.

The baby's head is pressed against Ma's neck while she hums an old hymn, a dwindling tune that creeps up and down the scales in a lazy, sweeping motion. The vibration of it against Hannah's face puts her into a daze. The tune is an old one that I recognize from when I was a child. The baby's jaw slacks open, and she makes low, flat hooting sounds.

Thickened spittle oozes from the corner of Hannah's mouth as she stares through me and through the rest of the world. It soaks into the shoulder of Ma's dress, and I shudder at the knowledge that I wish her dead.

Ma motions for Joanna and Charles to scram after the baby's eyes finally begin to roll back in her head. Her eyelids have sunk into sleepy half-moons, a sure sign that she'll be out soon. The children and I leave the cabin quietly, careful not to stomp our feet upon the hard wood of the floor panels. I set Ma's Bible in her free hand before I go, and she mouths me a silent thanks.

"Are you sure you're all right, daughter?" she whispers again, but I wave her off with a small smile. *Leave me alone, Ma. Nobody can help me now.*

As soon as I step outside and close the door, the forest begins to echo with the sound of the children's excited yells as they chase each other through the trees.

Emily calls out for Charles to be careful after he slips on a patch of pine needles and nearly collides with a mossy tree stump.

I tell Emily that I need to do my business and make my way around the opposite side of the cabin. When I'm sure she's stopped looking nervously after me, I loop around to an especially twisted tree trunk, once alive but now blackened and gnarled by a lightning bolt that nearly caused our cabin to burn down when I was ten.

I lift a rogue shrub branch from its resting place at the foot of the tree. Sure enough, a peppermint-flavored candy stick is tucked beneath. Its shiny finish, perfect white-and-red swirls that drip down the length of the sweet beneath twists of waxed paper, is stark and brilliant against the dark, muddy earth. A red ribbon is tied carefully around its middle.

Henry is already here, waiting for me in our secret place, no doubt with a blanket strewn over the dead leaves and needles of the forest floor. My hand finds itself over my lower belly before I even realize what's happening. The very thought of telling Henry about the baby is staggering, but it's something that I know I must do if I want him to consider marrying me.

"Come here, sister!" Emily calls to me from the forest once I return from the dead tree, the sweet in my pocket. Her face is smiling, and her cheeks are rosy from chasing Joanna and Charles. "The children have decided that they want a new pet. We should find something furry and pleasant before they set their minds on a snake again!"

I slide my hand into the pockets of my skirts and wrap my fingers around the peppermint stick. I cannot risk showing up too late and having Henry be gone already.

I cannot make it another fortnight.

"Apologies, Emily." I make a vague gesture around my middle, then point to the trees behind me. "I think that maybe I will take a walk instead. Some fresh air, perhaps, for my stomach."

The disappointment shines in her dark eyes. The corners of her mouth turn down, and she crosses her arms. "Shouldn't you feel like resting after what happened this morning?"

"I feel well enough," I say. "Just need to breath, I think. Enjoy the silence."

"Right." Her voice is cold. She is upset that I would rather be alone than be with her. I wish I could tell her the truth. "See you when you return then, I suppose."

And she turns away.

The idea that this is how it ends, this is the last conversation I will have with my sister before I run away to give birth like an animal in hiding, is more than I wish to endure. I want to hug her, promise her I'll come back for her, lie to her that everything will be well and that

I'm only going on a journey to find her a better dearest friend.

I don't, of course. Instead, I walk away from my sister without even saying goodbye.

THREE

My meeting place with Henry is about a quarter mile from the cabin, and I trudge through the woods with my skirts gathered near my waist so I can move faster through the fallen branches and shrubs and tangled vines.

The struggle to keep Emily's face from my mind is terrible. She is going to be so very worried about me when I fail to return. She'll likely torture herself for years with hundreds of different visions of possible ways to die during a walk in the woods, each one worse than the one before, until she's finally forced to move forward and let me go.

You know she never will.

Still, though, one day I'll simply turn up for her. I try to picture what her face will look like then, instead of how it did just now.

It's still early enough for the lingering mist of the mountain's morning to swirl lazily around the trees and blur the edges of the world like a dream. Usually I take much more time with the walk, to enjoy the peace and beauty of the mountainside and savor the excitement over seeing Henry, but right now I can't even bring myself to consider the spicy smell of wildflowers or the scattered flurry of squirrel feet dashing across the leaves.

I am with child, I imagine myself saying to Henry. *We are to be mother and father.*

Whatever it is that means.

In my imagination, Henry rejoices at the news and promises to take care of us both. He tells me that he's been hoping this would happen. He tells me that he wants to be married immediately. He tells me that God loves all his children, no matter how they come about, even if not under his holy matrimony.

I pull out half of the broken peppermint stick from my pocket and begin to suck at the end of it. The sweet mint flavor is Heaven on my tongue, settling to my stomach, and also calms my nerves until I come to the clearing by the creek. When I emerge, I can see that Henry's horse, General, is tied up against a tree near the water. He drinks it up in big, loud gulps, but Henry is nowhere to be seen.

The blanket that we usually lie upon is settled over the dirt in the same spot as always. The memory of us entangled on the blanket, thrusting against each other and crying out in pleasure, causes my chest to flush with warmth beneath my calico dress. With the excited feeling comes the usual guilt, the automatic force that seeps into the good feelings and stains them like ink. *Filth. Selfish filth.*

Have I truly been ruined?

"Henry?" I call out softly. My eyes scan the woods behind General. "I have something to tell you, darling."

My heart startles at the feeling of his hands suddenly around my waist from behind, pulling me back into him, and the front of his pants is already bulging.

"Hello, my love," he whispers into my ear with that rough, eager voice. "I would be lying if I said I wasn't envious of that candy in your mouth."

I need to be solemn, but the hungry manner of his speaking causes me to laugh. I cannot help it.

"Oh, really?" I say and withdraw the candy. I spin around to face him, and now his bulge is pressed against my groin. His hands wander wildly over my backside. "Want a taste, then?"

And he's kissing me now, deep and long with sugary bursts of peppermint. I let him, to draw him in, to make this easier on myself. I need him to want me. His hands leave my backside and find themselves groping my sore breasts with vigor. I wince at the pressure.

"Take this cursed dress off." He pulls away from my mouth long enough to make the demand before he starts tasting my ear, my neck, my collarbone. "I cannot wait to have you today."

"It pleases me to hear such enthusiasm," I say in a coy tone. I push away from him and sit on the blanket.

"Why aren't you undressing?" he asks after a moment and sinks down next to me. His hands fly to the buttons on his own trousers, but I stop him.

"I need to ask you something."

I start sucking on the candy again, to calm my scorching nerves, and this time Henry doesn't appear as excited about it. He waits without a word.

"Do you love me?" I ask. "You say it every time we're together. I just wanted to know if it is true or not."

"Of course it's true!" he almost bursts, and starts fumbling with his pants again. He lets out a sigh of relief. "I thought you were going to ask me something serious."

"How would you feel if I told you that you are to be a father?"

I say it with closed eyes so that I can be spared his immediate reaction. I hear him stop messing with his trousers, finally, and now his breath is quickening even more than it was when he was grabbing at me.

"What?" he asks.

His voice is pure panic. Not excitement, not joy. Fear. Confusion. Panic.

"Because you are," I finish, and I put my hand over my stomach on impulse for the hundredth time that day. "I am with child."

I observe his face carefully. It shows no emotion at all, but at least there isn't a scowl.

"You are—" Henry leans his elbows against his knees and runs his hands through his thick, straw-colored hair "—with child."

"I know it's a shock," I say and reach for his hand. I wrap my fingers around his palm, but he doesn't return with any sort of squeeze. "I'm not ecstatic about it myself, exactly. But my family...they cannot find out, Henry. Not now, not before we've been wed. Do you have any idea what my pa would think about this?"

"What do I care about your pa?" he snaps and looks at me, his expression cold. "And you won't be able to hide it for long. I can't do anything about *that*." He doesn't mention my comment about marriage.

Perhaps he didn't hear me.

I think back to my fantasy about Henry's reaction, and my stomach begins to feel queasy again. The sweet mint taste that coats my throat becomes metallic.

"Unless..." I say and hold on to the last bit of hope in my heart. "Unless we go away together."

"What?" Henry cries and stands upright. "Are you mad, Amanda? I cannot care for an infant! I cannot care for a *wife*!"

"Maybe you don't think so now," I say and get up after him. "But you could do it, Henry, I know you could. We could get married and—"

"And what, Amanda?" His voice is raised now, birds are scattering around us, and he begins folding the blanket back up as if he has somewhere very important to be. "I didn't think this would happen. I didn't *want* this to happen."

Henry has changed into a little child looking for a place to flee, and it fills me with such anger. How dare he act as if I've done it to myself? He looks around nervously and shoves his hands into his pockets before I step forward.

"You wanted it whenever your parts needed a good tugging," I accuse. "You never seemed to worry about it then."

My voice is dripping with poison, bitter and panicked and over-the-top. Who have I become? This is helping nobody, least of all myself. "Listen, Henry, let me apologize. I'm just— I thought you said you loved me." My lip quivers, and now I'm a child just like him.

"I did," Henry says and drapes the blanket over the back of General's saddle. "But I didn't ask for this."

"Please, don't go," I cry and fall to my knees. I clasp my hands as if in prayer. "Please, Henry. Please, take me with you. *My family cannot find out about—*"

"Your baby," he says, more to himself than me, as he looks down at my streaming face and runny nose in disgust. "It's *your* baby. You'll just have to find a way to tell them."

"It is ours!" I bellow and get off my knees. I run up to Henry, start slapping his broad chest with my hands, and he grabs my wrists and fights me off. "Don't you

do this to me, Henry! Don't you dare leave me here. I'll
be disowned! They'll...they'll..."

"Stop it, Amanda!"

"You said that you loved me," I repeat over and over,
and now I feel as though I'm watching all of this from
the outside instead of being in it. "Why has your heart
turned in such a manner?"

"Listen," Henry says. "I enjoyed you a lot, Amanda.
You came into town with your pa that one day to use
my post, and I couldn't take my eyes off you. I would
have continued doing this for as long as you wanted. I
would have."

He mounts General in a smooth, sweeping motion,
something that used to make him look handsome and
strong and dreamy to me, something that now makes
him look like a coward, a deserter of war. I try to hug
General's neck to keep him close, but Henry makes a
small, urgent click with his tongue and leads the horse
right through the creek. The cold water splashes over
my ankles as they pass, but I hardly notice.

"Henry—" I start to protest as he rides away, but then
I hear some sort of excitement behind me, a sudden
crunch of twigs and leaves too loud to have been made
by a squirrel or even a raccoon. Fear sparks to life in
my chest.

Is it a wolf? A bear? How fitting it would be for me
to get attacked and torn apart right here and now, just

like I wanted my family to think happened when I ran away. Perhaps it's a reckoning for me.

Or, perhaps...it's the creature again.

With a racing heart and trembling lips, I turn to face the noise. My fists are clenched, although I don't intend to fight. I open my eyes, ready to be devoured.

Oh, this is a reckoning, all right. Because it's not a wolf or a bear or the devil standing on the opposite side of the clearing, staring at me with completely wild eyes and an open mouth.

It's Emily.

It's Emily, and from the look on her face and the way she turns to run away from me, I can tell that she's heard and seen everything.

FOUR

I sprint after her, calling her name, bellowing for her to stop so I can explain. She doesn't stop or even look over her shoulder as she jumps over logs and dodges trees and bushes. I try to keep up, but the tightening in my belly and the gentle sear of pain across my groin slows me before I've even made it fifteen paces.

"Stop!" I yell again, and when that doesn't work I give it one last try before I collapse on my knees in the dirt. *Say whatever it takes to make her stop.* "Let me explain! You owe it to me—"

That does it. Emily slides to a halt in the dead leaves and turns back to look at me, her delicate face twisted in fury. Before I can get up from the ground, she's in front of me.

"Please—" I start, but I am cut off when Emily winds up and slaps me across the face, hard.

The blow knocks me back. The side of my face is buzzing, and my ear is on fire.

"*I* owe it to *you*?" Emily cries. Her hands are twitch-
ing at her side. Sweat glistens in small beads over her
reddened face. "I owe you nothing! What have you done
to yourself, Amanda? And how? *Why?*"

I don't know where to begin. Because I'm no longer
the sister that she once knew, perhaps? What would
Emily think of me to discover that I pray for the death
of baby Hannah so that Ma won't have to? None of it
makes sense to me except that I feel broken and cor-
rupt, and because of that it was distracting and freeing
to have such an intimate thing all to myself.

Before last winter, Emily and I didn't have things to
ourselves, not from each other anyway, and because
of that, nothing I can say right now will make her less
upset with me. *Selfish filth.*

"The lie never went away, did it?" Emily says. There
is a brief pause. "At the end of the spring, you told me
you were better. And now—"

"I was better, of course I was!" I cross my arms at her
arched brow. "I *am*. I didn't mean to hurt you, sister," I
say earnestly and mean it. I pull at the end of my braid.
"This is all a mistake."

I curse Henry in my mind for leaving me here, for
forcing me to have this conversation with Emily now.
I curse myself for taking something unbreakable with
my sister and finding a way to shatter it into pieces. My
sister sinks to the forest floor beside me.

"You were going to leave." She says it in a near whisper, soft with a deadly undertone. "You were going to *leave* me here, you were just going to *run away* with some boy that apparently came out of nowhere. Really, Amanda, how did you even meet him? I didn't even know you *knew* any boys."

She laughs now, a sad and empty laugh, then wipes away a tear with a nod of astonishment. "So really, I do not know you at all. I do not know anything. You were going to leave me."

Emily looks down. "It was as if the winter was only a warning for what was to come."

I think of the past few months, of lying to Emily's face so that I could be filled with Henry and feel ecstatic and in control and *alive*, of telling myself that I would stop when I knew deep down that I had no intention to. I think of the moment I first knew I was with child.

"Our lives were already falling to pieces without this, this—" Emily fades away and begins pulling weeds and pieces of grass from the ground. "This bastard child."

Bastard. The word hits me like a dirty curse and sends my heart into a panic. My baby will be a bastard. An earthworm sprawls over itself in the freshly turned soil. *It's unfair*, I consider as I watch it try to burrow back down. *It has no way of comprehending what is happening to it. It thinks it might die.*

"I don't know what I'm going to do," I admit to myself for the first time, and cover my face with my hands. "I have ruined everything."

"You have," Emily agrees. "You truly, truly have. Ma and Pa are going to be sick over it."

Just the idea of trying to inform Ma and Pa of their soon-to-be grandchild is enough to turn my guts into mush. I hug myself and start to rock back and forth.

"Please, don't tell them, Emily," I beg. "I need to do it. At the right time."

Emily doesn't bother to scold me that there is no right time for this particular announcement, even though I can tell she's biting her tongue. She shrugs and lets out an aggravated sigh.

"I would never," she says finally. "I wouldn't wish such a task upon anybody, much less myself."

"Thank you, sister." I study her for any sign of possible reconciliation, but there is none. "I'm truly grateful for that."

"Don't be," she says. "You won't be grateful when you are reaping the consequences from what you've done."

I start to cry, and Emily's eyes scour my face in silence for a few moments.

"You've changed," she whispers, and leans away from me to stand up. "This isn't you."

We start back toward the cabin after that, and Emily ignores me for the entire walk, staying at least ten strides ahead at all times. I want to tell her everything, about Hannah and Henry and the wanting to sin, but every time I speak she makes a point not to look at me or respond in any way.

Before long, the roof of our cabin becomes visible through the trees. The smoke from the chimney drifts up in wispy billows and sets the air alive with the smell of fire. Joanna and Charles are still gathered in the front clearing, playing with a toad and cheering and whooping as though nothing in this life is sour or wrong.

"Ma was looking for you, Amanda," Joanna calls when she sees Emily and me emerging from the forest. "Something about Hannah."

I start for the cabin, but Emily stops me.

"Amanda."

I turn back, hopeful, desperate, and look into my sister's eyes.

"I just want you to know something," she says in a low voice.

"Yes?"

"I don't know if I'll ever be able to forgive you for this," Emily admits. "Ever."

FIVE

I am alone again.

I feel as though there is always a buzz in the air, reminding me that reality has changed, that life right now might as well all be a nightmare. Emily stays true to her word and doesn't mention the baby to Ma or Pa, and neither do I. Since I didn't think they'd ever have to find out, I hadn't even explored options on how to break the news, but after only a few days I decide that I will never tell them, I will just allow them to notice one day and then finally admit to my doings.

Or perhaps I can pretend that I don't know how it happened?

The days pass like molasses in the winter. Pa makes weekly trips to the settlement on the other side of the mountain to trade his furs for supplies, and Ma and I tidy up the cabin or prepare the upcoming meal or read Bible passages to calm ourselves while Hannah wails with fits of incredible rage all throughout the day.

Since the disastrous conversation with Henry, I've been keeping inside with Ma during any free time instead of going on walks with the children and Emily. It sort of becomes an unspoken agreement between my sister and me; we are civil to each other when required in front of our ma and pa, but other than that, we are nothing more than strangers who sleep in the same bed. I grieve for our sisterhood more and more with every ignored attempt to set things right between us.

Besides the heavy heart I always carry about Emily, I am also ever paranoid that Ma is going to sense that I'm with child, because aren't mothers naturally equipped with a deep intuition about such things? And especially since she's been making a point to pay closer attention to me after what happened last winter, like she blames herself for it, somehow.

Before the day has even begun, Hannah has fallen into a full-body tantrum. I can't help but wonder why the Lord would want to put an infant through such anguish; what is the greater purpose of it, truly? With every day, the answer becomes less clear.

I keep praying for you to die, I think in shamed dismay as Hannah screams and writhes on the mattress, despite Ma's every effort to calm her with the tip of her breast. A twinge in my belly brings tears to my eyes.

Pa is up before dawn to make another settlement run, and raises his voice over the baby to promise Joanna and Charles that he'll bring them each a special treat upon his return, on account that it will be Joanna's birthday soon and there won't be another trip in until after it has passed.

Hannah doesn't quiet down until he has been gone for an hour or two.

The children spend the day buzzing around like excited chickens, leaving Ma to Hannah and Emily and I to engage in our separate chores. Neither of us rush in an attempt to gather free time like we usually do, and Emily takes special care to make her daily chores stretch out the entire day. In the afternoon, it begins to rain.

Pa returns just as the sun is setting, dripping with mud and rainwater. He ties Rocky up to the post by the woodshed and starts unloading things—soap, cornmeal, molasses, fresh herbs and spices for Ma. Joanna waits for her gift at the table. She tugs impatiently at the end of her raven curls, the anticipation making her eyes widen by the minute.

Once Rocky is having his supper along with our other horse, Blackjack, and Pa has changed into dry clothes, he sits across from Joanna and produces a doll made from a dried corncob. It has no hair, just a dress made with scrap pieces of calico fabric that wrap around the lower half, and a blank-looking face set in with beans. My little sister couldn't be happier.

Jo squeals in delight and runs to Pa, but I notice as he hugs her that something isn't quite right with his face. He is smiling at Joanna's excitement, but trouble lurks beneath his placid expression. Ma and Emily must sense it, too, because neither of them go out of their way to ask how his trip was.

After Joanna retreats to the back corner to play with her new doll, Pa pulls out a painted spinning top for Charles and offers it with a weak smile. Charles's jealous frown dissolves in a moment, and soon he is sitting beside his sister testing out his new toy.

"I have some hard news to go over with you, Susan," Pa says. "Amanda and Emily, you might as well hear this, too."

My heart jumps into my throat. Perhaps he's received bad news of one of our aunts or cousins from the settlement at the base of the mountain? Pa motions for us to sit around the table with him, so we all do, and wait quietly for him to begin speaking. Just before he begins, I have a flash of panic where I think, *What if he knows about the baby?*

"This winter is going to be bad." Pa finally speaks after folding his hands in front of him on the table. He doesn't look into our faces. "Very bad."

"What do you mean, Edmund?" Ma says. Her voice is gentle, afraid, and she gets up to set a sleeping Hannah on her bed.

"I heard it while I was at the settlement today," he says after she sits back down. "The farmers can all see it, clear as day. Apparently there's a big ring around the moon, normal for autumn, but not this thick or this bright. Everyone was buzzin' about it from the moment I got in. It marks a hard winter ahead." He pauses. "The worst we've ever had, maybe."

Worse than last year, is what he's trying to say without saying it. How is that even possible?

"Excuse me for being so bold, Pa," Emily says and shrugs ever so slightly. "But why can't we simply stock up on supplies to better prepare this time? We've had to deal with much harder things than snow before."

How vast an understatement.

"Do you think I have forgotten about last winter, Emily?" Pa's voice rises. I notice from the corner of my eye that Joanna and Charles are both casting glances my way. When I turn to look at them, they quickly avert their eyes. "Any one of us could get ill like Ma did again, and with no safe way to travel for help. With this many people, it is too dangerous, plain and simple. There are seven of us living in a cabin built for three."

Soon to be eight, I think, and Emily stares at me from across the table. I know she's thinking the same thing.

Nobody speaks. I imagine being trapped in the cabin with my family when the discovery is made that I am with child. I imagine having nowhere to go to escape their wrath. I imagine giving birth and screaming in pain and losing my mind inside a cramped cabin of stale air and baby wails and arguing children.

Perhaps, with any luck, I won't survive the delivery.

Pa gets up to take a peek at the storm after a low but

heavy roll of thunder causes the inside of my ears to hum. "Even traveling in the rain here is difficult now," he says, and closes the door to the cabin. "It didn't used to be this way. We'd have one hard snow, maybe two, never amounting to anything more than a couple of lazy days inside."

"You're right," Ma agrees. Her face is pale. "It seems as though each winter has gotten gradually worse."

"There is only one thing we can do to protect ourselves," Pa says and turns from the window. "We will need to settle elsewhere."

"Elsewhere?" I say. "Are you talking about the settlement at the foot of the mountain? Where Aunt Charlotte lives?"

My chest tightens at the thought. While it sounds much better than spending the winter in the cabin, being surrounded by even more familiar faces to witness my downfall doesn't seem all that wonderful either. At least there'd be room to breathe.

"No," Pa says, and I exhale a small sigh of relief. "We need somewhere large enough to comfortably house all of us. This place is already too cramped, and it's bigger than most of the cabins on or around the mountain. There isn't enough time to build a new one, besides. No, I think we need to move someplace very different."

"Like where?" Ma says what I am thinking.

Pa sits in silence for a few moments. "There is a big

stretch of free land to the far south," he says. "It's a great distance away from the mountain—"

"Great distance?" Ma repeats with a hand over her chest. "Oh, Edmund. I can't leave behind my sister, and her children..."

"You can, and you will," Pa insists. Ma lets out a sigh and lowers her hand back down to her lap. "This is for the greater good of our family, Susan. I was told that this land is riddled with abandoned cabins. I wouldn't even have to build a new one."

"That would save quite a bit of time," Ma agrees, then pauses to ponder. I see her look toward Hannah, then at me. Her cheeks deepen in color, and the corners of her mouth turn down. "I think we should leave, too. I don't want for there to be a chance that last year could happen again."

"It *won't*," Pa says and hits his fist on the table suddenly, causing Ma to jump. "Now, I've told you all plenty of times, and after this it is no longer up for conversation—everybody needs to forget about last winter. All of you continue to draw out the misery instead of choosing to recognize that the Lord blessed us all with survival. We could have so easily lost Ma and Hannah, but we didn't."

He is purposefully leaving me out of it, just like the few other times he has tried to have this talk with us. Ma and Emily look uncomfortably into their laps. I realize that Pa may never treat me like he did before the storm again. It's been months, and he still refuses to acknowledge my incident.

Is he ashamed? Or is he afraid?

"The cabin is too small for seven people," he repeats now, and clears his throat. "It wasn't healthy for any of us to be so close to each other for so long. It will not happen again, and you all need to forget about it. Thank the merciful Lord for what you have now."

What I really "need" to forget about is Henry. Maybe going away will be a blessing. No more worries about bad winters, more room, a fresh start away from the monster post boy. Maybe being somewhere new will make the news of my baby easier for Ma and Pa to swallow.

Maybe.

Ma and Pa sit at the table, talking things through for a few hours. The idea of living anywhere but the mountain is so very strange to me. All I've ever known, all my siblings have ever known, is trees and mist and cool air and walls of rock.

When Joanna and Charles head to bed, each child with their new toy tucked protectively under their arms, I decide to follow suit rather than listen in on the exhausting conversation any longer.

"Amanda," Emily says when she sees me changing into my nightshirt. "Wait a moment, please."

She comes over to my side of the mattress after

double-checking to make sure Ma and Pa are still deep in their talk.

"What is it?" I ask.

Emily leans in close so she can whisper in my ear.

"Do not say anything about the baby yet," she says softly. "Wait until after we've settled."

"You think?" I whisper back, slightly amused at her change of heart. "But, Emily, *they have the right to know!*"

"Hush," she grumbles and makes her way over to the chest which contains her own nightshirt. "Obviously, the circumstances have changed."

"It's hard to believe we will be settling elsewhere," I say, eager for the chatter between us. "It will be strange to live somewhere so far away from the clouds and the trees."

But Emily just pulls her nightshirt over her head and climbs into bed next to Joanna without a word.

The rain has ceased by the next morning, and Pa rushes to pack things for the resettlement before the sun rises. Clearly we are wasting no time. Ma wakes us early so that we can help make breakfast before the day of especially hard work. She stirs cornmeal mush, while Emily goes out to pick blackberries and I twist hay into sticks for the fire.

Joanna and Charles are still sleeping deeply, unaffected by the cooking sounds and smells and urgent whispers of today's plans. Ma explains how Emily and

I will need to help her and Pa prepare the wagon for the trip. Almost all of our furniture will need to stay behind, she tells us. Pa will be able to make more at the new homestead, with the proper supplies, and the free room in the wagon will be better spent on supplies and clothes and tools for cooking and building.

"Should we also pack wood from the shed?" Emily suggests. "For fires?"

"Yes, the wood," Ma says while she mixes the mush in a large bowl. It steams around her hands as though laced with magic. "I'd forgotten. We will need to bring some of it along, as well."

Pa moves back and forth between the cabin and the stables, collecting his tools and rifles and bullet pouches into different piles on top of the tarp that lies outside the front door. He fills an empty sack with utensils and trinkets and other small items of the like, and already the cabin is beginning to look emptier.

When I go to the stables to give Pa his breakfast, I notice that his purchase consisted of much more than usual, proof that he decided upon this move long before leaving the settlement yesterday. For somebody who insists the Lord would never let the events of last winter repeat themselves, he sure seems afraid of the possibility.

Hidden beneath an oiled canvas to protect it from rain are stacks and stacks of dried meat strips, bulging bags of dried corn and wheat and spices, salt pork, turnips, molasses, dried fruit, jars of jelly. I marvel at the amount of food, run my hands over the jars and bags and wrappings.

"We'll need it all," Pa says from behind me. I turn to hand him the bowl of blackberry-topped corn mush and a tin cup filled with coffee. "The trip will be very long. I traded some of my father's gold to arrange for there to be an ox at the foot of the mountain to help share the load with the horses."

He speaks without looking upon my face.

"I've never ridden in the wagon before," I observe aloud as I look at the pile of assorted wooden parts for it. "None of us have."

"You'll be walking behind the wagon for most of the trip," Pa says in between big bites, his voice quiet and distant like it always is with me now. "There won't be enough room left to ride comfortably for long periods of time." When the bowl is empty, he hands it to me without meeting my eye and motions me away.

When breakfast is through, the work begins. The large, hickory bows that will be erected for the canvas over the top of the wagon are piled together behind stacks of feed grass, and we pull out the large curves of wood and line them up in the front clearing.

Ma joins Emily and me to help spread a strong-smelling oil over the huge white wagon canvas, a task that will protect the wagon's contents from water damage in case we should travel through rain. It takes the entire day for us to assemble the hickory bows over the wagon and stretch the canvas over the top, then pack as much as we possibly can into the bed of the wagon.

We will be abandoning our cabin in the morning.

Before going to bed, Pa goes over the plan for tomorrow. Before dawn we will rise, eat a quick breakfast of dried meat and pan biscuits, and head to the bottom of the mountain as carefully and quickly as possible. Ma will ride in the front of the wagon with Pa, holding Hannah, and Joanna and Charles will sit in the back of the wagon until we reach the foot of the mountain.

Emily and I will walk behind the wagon to watch for potential wheel breaks or other problems. Once we've reached the bottom, Pa says, we'll be able to push forward to our new home at a much quicker pace. According to the men in the settlement, if we head down a certain line of forest for long enough, we'll come across an array of abandoned cabins to claim one as our own. Pa expects that we'll be able to find someplace within a fortnight.

"There is a surprise waiting for us at the bottom," he concludes, just to pique the interest of Joanna and Charles, who have spent the last half of the afternoon crying and saying goodbye to everything in sight—trees, rocks, the grave of their pet toad that got its bowels hollowed out by a coyote a few nights ago. Pa must be talking about the ox. "A very exciting surprise."

We fall asleep early, and in the morning after we've

risen and dressed and eaten, we begin our journey to the bottom of the mountain. Emily and I walk behind the wagon as planned while Pa leads it down carefully, steering the horses in long, slow curves that keep it from tumbling out of control with speed.

I turn back to look after my old home, my old life, only one time. Early morning mists swirl over the front clearing of the cabin as the sound of hungry birds peppers the air with cheeps. The air is damp and earthly sweet. I am bombarded by the memory of Emily and me playing with each other as children, whispering secrets and singing songs and telling ghost stories around the fire pit outside.

Dearest friends forever, we'd promise each other. *Forever and a day.*

Resettlement or not, those days are over. Emily will never think of me as her home again. I think of the part of me that died here last winter, the part that will dwell within the cabin, like a ghost, and wait for Emily to come back. But she never will, of course.

The ghost will be forever waiting.

"Goodbye," I whisper to the memories, to Henry, to the cabin.

"Goodbye," I whisper to the lost part of myself.

SIX

From afar, the abandoned prairie cabin appears to be very large. It is at least three times the size of our old one, a giant roofed rectangle of log stacks that sits randomly on the stretch of endless flat grasses. Jackrabbits the size of small coyotes hop around in scattered clusters over the landscape, their ears amusingly oversize.

Pa whoops at the sight of them, and I wonder just how much rabbit stew a single one of those creatures would create. We haven't eaten stew or anything heartier than dried fruits and nuts for over a week now. Traveling didn't go quite as quickly as Pa planned due to the extra heavy load, two broken wheels, and the reality of how long it took to set up and break down camp for a family of seven twice each day. So he stopped hunting to cut back on wasted time.

All of the animals survived, and we've managed to avoid illness, though, so I suppose that in itself is another true-to-blue Verner family miracle. For twenty days we traveled, we camped, we ate hastily prepared turnips and leathery meat strips and drank woody water from the rain barrel. Our clothes, even while dry, are completely rotted with sweat, and the fabric feels as though it is stiffened with wax against our ever-damp skin.

From the foot of the mountain, the rolling grassy hills lined with bushes eventually leveled themselves out before transforming to an endless stretch of prairie lands, covered with tall grasses and sizzling in the sun.

The first cabin we came upon was occupied by a family with three small children, who waved to us like ants on the horizon as we passed the area from a distance. The second one was empty, but smaller than our mountain cabin and riddled with holes and unfilled gaps between the logs. By the time we discover the third, everybody is cross and desperate for the journey to end.

Please, let this be the one, I think as I wipe the sweat from my eyebrows. *I don't think I can take this much longer.*

I try to remember the point where the grasses went from short and thick to tall and willowy, but for the life of me I cannot. I am so tired, and my feet hurt so much from walking that I've had to ride in the back of the wagon with the children for the past few days, while Emily rode Blackjack to lead Rocky and the ox while they pulled.

I am no more used to the idea of a baby inside of me than I was before we left the mountain.

Pa, Ma and Hannah sat on the front bench for nearly the entire ride. The bumps and sudden jerks that the wagon took were uncomfortable for the rest of us, but seemed to relax the baby more than she'd ever been before, and I am glad that at least Hannah is feeling at ease with the conditions.

The prairie seems to go on forever, into the startling blue sky embellished with fluffy white clouds, except for a dense stretch of forest that begins about a mile to the south. The sight of the trees is comforting, as it reminds me of home. If I ever find myself missing the mountain, I could just go to that forest and pretend, even for a little while, that I was back there again.

From this distance there appears to be a fence wrapped around the front of the desolate cabin, and I know that Ma is probably very pleased about that. I think of our cozy cabin cradled high in the mountains, with the front clearing that was raked and lined with smooth white stones.

"Wow," Emily breathes from on top of Rocky, just outside the wagon where I'm sitting with the children. "It's so large!"

"See?" Pa turns around in the wagon to smile at us, relief softening his eyes for the first time since before we left the mountain. "I told you the Lord would provide!"

"We don't know yet if this is the one," Ma says flatly. "We're only seeing it from afar, and it could be in ruins."

"Oh, nonsense," Pa insists. "Nothing that a few repairs can't take care of. Everybody, welcome to our new homestead!"

Ma frowns. I can't help but wonder that if at any point, between the disappointment of the second cabin and the children beginning to cry every night about their hatred for camping, perhaps Pa had considered that taking the word of a couple of farmers about how much opportunity this land held might not have been the cleverest idea.

Joanna and Charles begin to cheer at the mention of the word *homestead*. Blackjack and Peter, the ox, gain a sudden burst of energy, as if they know that their bones will *finally* be able to properly rest if they just finish it now, and the wagon begins to glide effortlessly through the prairie. As we gain speed we begin to bump, softly at first but increasingly violently as the wheels tear over animal holes and thick bunches of field grass. I fold my arms over my middle in an effort to keep things as still as possible.

"Slow down," Ma nearly yells and throws her hand over the upset sunbonnet on her head. "It's not going anywhere."

"It's beautiful, isn't it?" Pa cries out in response, without slowing down. "At last, at last!"

But the dreamy vision of the cabin fades as we draw closer. It becomes painfully clear when we pull up that the yard and surrounding area are in need of some se-

rious work. The bark from the logs is peeling away from
the wood as if the cabin is shedding. Weeds have over-
grown everything, spreading hungrily over the ground,
the bottom perimeter of the cabin, even covering an old
busted wheelbarrow that sits behind the fence.

The fence itself is more of just a frame, really. Long
pieces of broken wood tilt diagonally away from the
posts and disappear into the grasses below. Extra pieces
are piled nearby, though not nearly enough to finish
the project, also covered in weeds. Sweat rolls down
my neck and soaks into the collar of my already ruined dress.

"Beautiful, indeed," Ma remarks. "It looks like nobody has lived here for years."

"The weeds grow quickly out here, Susan." Pa sighs,
clearly aggravated at her lack of fervor. He pulls the
reins in, and Blackjack and Peter slow to a stop in front
of the new cabin. "They'll only take one good workday
to get rid of. And I'll be able to scrape all that bark off
with my draw knife, and re-clay the gaps between the
logs..."

Joanna and Charles jump from the wagon as soon
as it stops. They run around the new yard like wild
ones, cheering and screaming with their arms flap-
ping around their heads. A couple of nearby rabbits
flee in a wide-eyed frenzy. I get out and stretch gratefully, careful to hide my swollen abdomen away from
my parents so they don't take notice.

Let this be my place to start anew, I think as I look again to the horizon of trees. *For me and for the baby.*

I stop.

The baby, not *my* baby. Even in my deepest thoughts I cannot feel grateful for it, and this fills me with shame.

"Who cares if we have to fix it up, Ma?" Emily says from behind me, pulling me from my thoughts. She heads through the weeds to the front door of the cabin. "Look at the size of it!"

Ma and I follow Emily while Pa tends to the animals, eager to see the inside, as well. Hannah sits on Ma's hip, lowering her hands to glide over the tips of the grasses poking up from below. As we approach the door, it's difficult to ignore the putrid stench that seems to be growing heavier with each step.

"Ugh," I say and pinch my nose. "What *is* that?"

It's too much for Hannah. She begins to scream, clawing into the air as if she wants to swim out of Ma's arms and away from the door, and we're forced to wait in the odor while Ma runs to set the baby in the back of the wagon so she can crawl around over the blankets.

Emily doesn't even look at me.

The sun pounds down on us and the prairie, and I realize that never in my life have I bore witness to weather this hot. And isn't it supposed to be autumn right now? I wonder if the stench is a dead animal roasting somewhere in the staggering heat. Hopefully the body isn't inside the cabin.

Ma rejoins us, and her face twists up again in reaction to the smell. She steps in front of Emily and opens the front door. The sight that greets us is silencing. My stomach breaks out in gooseflesh, despite the sweltering heat.

The cabin's hardwood floor has been completely torn out, and pokes jaggedly inward at the edges. Weeds and dirt and dead grass floor the entire inside, and the light from the open doorway prompts dozens of grasshoppers to fly through the air. Various pieces of furniture, most of them broken, lay scattered over the ground.

There is a dark substance, a stinking liquid that covers the entire edge of the torn out floor. Even as much as I don't want to believe it, I know that the liquid is, unquestionably, blood. There is more of it splattered up the sides of the peeling bark walls, and a broken chair amongst the wreckage is also ruined with the red. Fat black flies the size of coins buzz against the filthy glass window that lines the back wall.

As terrible as the sight is, as positively jarring, it is *nothing* compared to the smell. Emily and Ma and I recoil and groan, our arms over our faces as we peer into the mess of a cabin. It is the smell of rot, thick and warm, it is the unmistakable smell of death. And it is heavy.

"What in Heaven's name?" Ma manages.

"Why aren't you going inside?" Pa calls from the front

of the wagon, where he holds a bucket for Peter to drink from. "What's it like?"

"Come over here," Ma yells back. "See for yourself."

The edge to her voice causes Pa's smile to die away in a second. He steps over a piece of broken fence to meet us after checking on Hannah in the back of the wagon. His eyes squint in rage as he takes in the condition of the cabin.

"What in the Hell?" he growls, and Ma doesn't even scold him for the curse. He steps inside, and we all follow.

"What happened here?" Emily asks, her voice meek. I look to the nearest corner of the cabin only to find that it's been filled by pillars of dense spider webbing. "Pa, I think that this is blood. It looks like..."

"I know what it looks like," Pa snaps, his face flat. "Somebody must have slaughtered an ox or horse in here."

"But why would they do it inside?" Ma says. "This cabin is completely ruined! We cannot settle here."

"It's *not* ruined." Pa frantically begins picking up the old furniture, most of the pieces completely caked with the dried blood, and tossing them out the front door. "We can remove all of the soiled items, and remove the bark from the wall with my draw knife. And I'll build a new floor."

"With what supplies?" Ma challenges. "And what money?"

"I'll find a way to arrange it," Pa promises. "We can camp outside until I get it fixed. We're almost at the end of the map that was drawn for me on the mountain. The nearby settlement should only be a day or so away to the west. I can leave tomorrow."

"You don't even know if the settlement will be there!" Ma is starting to get teary. Emily and I remain silent. "They also said there would be 'plenty' of decent homesteads that were unoccupied, as well. Whoever drew up that map could have misremembered, they could be sending you out into the wilderness to die, or it could take you days—"

"*Susan.*" The tone of Pa's voice is dangerous enough to silence her outburst instantly. "You will camp outside with the children until I return, and then I'll fix the floor and the walls and you'll wonder what you ever had to complain about in the first place."

How heavy his desperation must be, if he is willing himself and the rest of us to accept the condition of this cabin. "It will be hard work," he continues, "but the Lord will smile upon us for it."

I watch Pa work to move the broken furniture out to be burned. Here is my new home, my place to begin clean, a place that is rotted and overheated and covered in filth. I've never heard of anybody slaughtering an animal inside their cabin before. It's almost fitting, in a sense.

I'm starting to believe that Hell is everywhere.

SEVEN

After he is finished purging the cabin of the soiled furniture, Pa moves the pieces to rest in a huge pile beside the cabin, declaring that he'll dig a trench to burn it all in during one of his next workdays. Then he cuts down enough grass for him, Emily, myself and Joanna to sleep on top of in the front yard. Charles, Ma, and Hannah will sleep in the wagon, where they are to be safe from whatever terrible creatures lurk around here at night.

I've never seen a rattlesnake, but I heard Pa talk about them on the way here, how you especially have to keep your eyes out when wading through the tall grasses, how they could strike a child's face or a horse's knee faster than the blink of an eye.

I don't like the idea of always being afraid of the snakes—the grasses are just so *tall*, everywhere, it's like we'll never be able to fully relax without worrying about somebody getting bitten and withering away from the deadly venom. I can hear a few rattles in the distance, none of them close, but they are unnerving all the same. I pray to God that they stay away from us.

Pa goes hunting for stew meat in the late afternoon, and returns only ten minutes later with one of the largest jackrabbits I have ever laid eyes upon. Its ears are so long that the body drags across the ground as Pa holds it at his side, the massive things bunched together inside Pa's huge fist. It's far less fat than a mountain rabbit, but will still provide at least twice the meat.

Ma attempts to start a cooking fire, but ends up nearly starting a blaze that could have claimed the entire prairie in under an hour.

"For God's sake, Susan!" Pa scolds, frantic, as he stomps out the quickly spreading flames that pour like fluid over the dried grass surrounding Ma's fire pit. He drops the jackrabbit in the excitement, and it lays in a grotesque pile, facedown, over the burnt grass. "You have got to be more careful out here! Dig a deeper pit and wet the edges with water from the barrel!"

Ma nearly bursts into tears. Coincidentally, Hannah begins howling from the back of the cabin just a moment later.

"You do it." Ma sniffs and turns away from Pa, dropping her spade into the dirt with a metallic *thunk*. "Hannah needs me." I expect Pa to scold her for dropping his tool, but he doesn't. After a frustrated sigh, he picks up the spade and starts working on the fire pit.

Ma walks to the wagon where Hannah is, her mouth

and eyes surrounded by ever-deepening wrinkles. I want to hug her so badly, but if I did that she would feel my belly sticking out from beneath my dress, and then Hannah would be the least of her worries. So when she passes by, I stay still.

*If only she could have just one day away from that baby...*I think. *Damn that baby. Damn that winter.*

I retrieve the twisted rabbit from its place on the ground and begin cutting away flesh from lean, tough muscle, and it feels wonderful, puts me at some ease, the sound of the flesh ripping, the crunch of broken cartilage. I almost wish I could do it forever.

Dinner is mostly silent, and then it's to bed for everybody. I can't decide what would be worse: sleeping inside that stinking cabin of spiders and flies or out here with the wild animals to devour us in the night.

Every time I close my eyes I imagine a snake burrowing in the foot of my blankets, or slithering across my throat while I sleep, and when I finally do manage to fall asleep it's all I can dream about, and I wake up feeling more tired than I was when I lay down.

After rigging up his old wooden cart from the wagon to Rocky, Pa leaves for the settlement early, promising to be back by sometime late in the night or early tomorrow morning. The moon is full, he says, and will light up the prairie just fine. He tells Ma again that everything will be fine. I can tell that Ma is nervous, and if

I'm being honest, so am I. How terrible would it be if Pa got lost and never came back?

After Pa has gone, the children play tag in the front clearing, whirling around the weeded fence posts and wheelbarrow and pile of wood. Ma rolls up all the blankets and makes a safe area for Hannah inside the wagon, then gives the baby a small rag to chew on and tug around.

"All right, girls," she says and straightens her back, looking to the forest that lines the south edge of the prairie. "It's time for us to find some water. There's still a bit left in the rain barrel, but not much, especially after Pa filled his canteens for the trip to town."

She looks back to the direction where he rode off and bites her lip. I can still see his silhouette on the horizon, but barely. I realize with a heavy stomach that he has the map, and if he were to perish, we would have no idea where to go for help.

"Anyway," Ma continues, "it's going to be very hard work."

"But where could we find any water around here?" Emily asks, her nose crinkled underneath her sunbonnet. "This place is dry as a bone."

"They wouldn't have built a home here if there wasn't water nearby," Ma says, not sounding entirely sure. "I don't see a well anywhere, so my next best guess is that you two will have to look for a creek in that forest back there. If you each took two buckets—"

Emily groans loudly in complaint, and my jaw almost drops in shock. Emily never sasses Ma or Pa, ever, that's always been my misgiving. And with the day Ma's been having, what is my sister thinking?

"If there's still water in the rain barrel, couldn't you allow us to rest for just one day before sending us out again, Ma?" Emily rubs her arms and pulls her mouth into a pained grimace. "My body is so very sore."

Something is amiss. I saw Emily lifting Charles into the air to spin him around not five minutes ago, and her arms didn't seem to hurt then. Her eyes meet mine again for just a second—unintentional, but I catch it, and now I know what she's doing.

She's trying to get us out of the work for *me*, not her. She must have observed how hard the trip has been on my body, despite my best efforts to hide it. It would be a lie to say that my stomach didn't turn with dread when Ma mentioned the forest.

I feel as though I'm about to fall apart.

I expect Ma to scold Emily and punish her—that's certainly what she would have done to *me* if I had been so bold—but instead she just turns her back to grab Hannah and mumbles something about doing what we please until it's time to prepare lunch. Upset at being picked up so suddenly, Hannah thrashes and screams against Ma's body. Ma hums a low, gentle tune, over and over and over, until the baby calms enough to press her face into Ma's throat to feel the vibrations.

"Thank you, sister," I whisper to Emily after I know Ma can't hear us. "I really appreciate—"

"Why are you thanking me?" my sister says, then starts walking toward Joanna and Charles. Emily calls out to them, wants to play with them, wants to get away from me. "I said that my body was hurting and I meant it."

If Ma notices that Emily's running and tagging with the children seems inconsistent with her woeful claim, she doesn't mention it. I think that she's reached her limit for the day already, all before it's even gotten a chance to begin. I mourn my ma's former happy self and wander away, so that there's less opportunity for her to pay attention to me and notice my belly.

I thought I would be braver by now, I thought that with time I'd grow more ready for my ma and pa to know about the baby, but I find myself just as afraid now as I was the day I realized I was with child.

I can't let them find out about this baby, I just can't. Oh, how I wish it could all go away.

I make my way around the side of the peeling cabin, inspecting it with disgust, terrified at the idea of giving birth here. I wonder again if I'll even survive the labor. Does dwelling on such morbid things make them more likely to happen in the future? Is praying for death blasphemous?

I'm removed from my thought when I round the back end of the cabin and see something sticking up through the grass—a cast-iron well pump. The new cabin has water access! It wouldn't be working now after being abandoned for so long, but maybe Pa can repair it once he gets back from that settlement. I step forward to inspect the well pump for any irreversible damage, and the smile from my discovery fades.

The grass and weeds directly around the pump have been torn away, and by the looks of it, somewhat recently. I take the pump handle in my hand and pull it up before pushing down. Cold water pours from the open spout and splashes into the dirt.

Someone has been to this cabin lately.

"Ma," I call around the corner, waving my hand. She makes her way over, careful to stay far enough from the cabin that Hannah won't scream in reaction to the smell. "Come, look at this."

"Praise the Lord," Ma gushes when she sees the well pump. She wipes the sweat from her forehead with her sleeve, and Hannah lets out a short yell. "Pa can get that in working order in no time—"

"That's just the thing, Ma," I say, and lean forward to grab the iron handle again. I pump it and more water rushes out. "It's already working."

"That's wonderful!" Ma cries, smiling for the first time in weeks. "What an improvement over hauling the rain barrel back and forth from the creek on the mountain, right?"

She doesn't seem the least bit suspicious, or even curious, as to how or why the well pump is working so well.

"Someone's been using this pump," I say slowly. "Isn't that a bad sign? Doesn't that mean that maybe this property is spoken for?"

Ma looks at me as though I am not speaking a language she understands. "You're asking if it's a bad thing that we found fresh water in the middle of this inferno of a flatland? Amanda, there isn't a soul to be seen around here for miles. It's just a blessing, is all. Nobody lives here, how could they? The inside of the—"

That's when someone steps out from behind the corner of the cabin. Since the figure is far too tall to be one of the children, my instinct wants to assume that it's Emily. I open my mouth to tell her about the well pump when I realize that it isn't Emily at all.

There is a boy with tanned leather trousers and a wide-brimmed hat standing in the grass, staring at us, unblinking.

He is holding a shotgun, and his hands are shaking.

EIGHT

One of the few things that Pa taught me about guns is that you don't hunt with a shotgun. You hunt with a rifle, which is used for accurate, long range control, the only type of gun that Pa owns. Shotguns have a more distinct and gruesome purpose: short-range annihilation. You use a shotgun when you want to take something's head off.

The boy's hands are still trembling. Ma gasps.

"P-please," she says, while Hannah presses her face into Ma's chest. The baby's features relax in fascination as she absorbs the thud of Ma's heartbeat. "My children..."

Inside of me, there is a terrible sort of mix. There is the panicking pulse of fear for our lives, but then there is also this hope, a strange hope, a morbid hope, that perhaps I won't have to see Ma's face when she finds out about Henry after all, won't have to endure the slaps to my face that Pa would carry out with a heavy hand.

Hope that perhaps I won't burn like this for eternity after my head is misted into oblivion.

"I won't shoot you," the boy says suddenly, as if he's only just now making that decision, as if he had to struggle with it. He takes a deep breath and glances to the window of the cabin. "I was— I didn't mean— I'm so sorry to have scared you. I was just shocked to see anybody here, that's all. My name is Ezekiel Jacobson, but my pa calls me Zeke."

"Where did you come from?" I ask. "Do you live here?"

Zeke looks in disgust at the peeling bark of the cabin's logs, the cracking and crumbling of the clay in between, the weeds around the bottom edges. "Of course not," he replies. "Haven't you looked inside?"

"Of course," Ma says, her hand over her stomach. "We've only just arrived to settle here. We didn't know anyone had claimed the land. My husband, Edmund, should be back any minute now..."

Ma is still afraid of the boy with the shotgun. She's probably wondering, as I am, why he's not holding a rifle instead, if he were hunting. By his reaction to the sight of us, it almost feels as though he *was* expecting somebody. Somebody else.

"This land isn't claimed, ma'am," Zeke says, his eyes shifting to the ground. "My pa and I live in those woods to the south—our cabin is only about a mile or so into the trees, so we're about two miles total from here.

We've just been running the well pump, is all. My pa, uh...he wouldn't be too happy at the idea of losing access to it. He's a doctor, and—"

The children scream from where they play in the front clearing, and Zeke looks quickly over his shoulder toward the sound. His grip around the gun tightens. "How many of you are there?"

"Seven total, including Edmund," Ma says quietly, still eyeing the shotgun. She shifts her weight. "Listen, I'm sure we could come to an agreement regarding the water..."

Zeke realizes now that my ma is still terrified of him. He sees her looking at his gun, he sees how hard she is trying to hold it together, and his eyes widen in surprise.

"Oh, no, ma'am," he says, and slowly slides the gun into a holster on his hip. His hands have stopped trembling. "I promise I am not here to do you any harm. I was just coming to gather some water, like I said—"

Just then Emily rounds the corner of the cabin, oblivious to the presence of the stranger. "Ma, the children are starting to ask for something to eat. Should I—"

That's when she sees Zeke. She takes a step back, her mouth open in a tiny O. "Who is this?"

"Where's your bucket?" I say to the boy, ignoring my sister's question. "You said you were coming to gather water, but you don't have anything to put it in."

"I..." Zeke blushes at the sight of Emily. Now that he's

not carrying the shotgun, I'm able to see that he looks to be about her age. "Wasn't there one next to the pump?"

"What water?" Emily says. "What pump?"

She spots the cast-iron well pump behind me. "Oh."

"There wasn't any bucket," I say. I do not want to let it go. I want to know who he was looking for, or who he was expecting.

"You said your pa is a doctor?" Ma asks, suddenly interested now that the gun is put away. "How many people are there in your family?"

Zeke frowns at the question. He sticks his hands into his pockets. "It's just my pa and me, ma'am. But he's a doctor, yes. He travels to Elmwood twice a week to see if anyone needs fixin'."

"Do you think he'd be willing to examine my baby?" Ma says. Her eyes are lit up, desperate at the opportunity, more alive than I've seen them in months. "I was ill when I had her. It caused her to be born blind and deaf, but there weren't any real doctors on our mountain, and all I want is for someone official to tell me that she isn't in pain, that she's scared but adjusting, that she'll be all right..."

She cuts off as if there is a lump in her throat. Her eyes are glassy.

"Of course," Zeke says gently. "I'll tell him about your baby as soon as I get home. You never mentioned your names, ma'am. Just that your husband's name is Edmund."

"Susan Verner," Ma says, and motions to the baby on her hip. "This is Hannah. And my daughters, Amanda and Emily."

Zeke smiles at Emily. "Lovely name, miss."

Emily grins, causing a wave of mild irritation to rise within me. She ought to be careful, that sister of mine. She has no idea what she could be getting herself into.

"The younger ones out front are Joanna and Charles," Emily says. Her voice is different than usual, smoother, more deliberate. Is she *flirting*? They'd better cut it out unless they want Ma to catch on to their little connection. A breeze brings the stench of the cabin into my nostrils for just a moment, and my stomach turns.

"How are you planning on living here, if you don't mind me asking?" Zeke's attention is back to Ma. "This place, it isn't fit for anyone. It hasn't been for years. Nobody really comes out here to—"

"What happened inside?" Ma asks. "Do you or your pa know? We thought that maybe someone had slaughtered a horse or ox in the cabin."

Zeke doesn't say anything for a moment, he just looks to the window of the cabin again. I want to mention the bucket once more, just to show that I am aware of his lie. It takes a liar to know one, maybe, but all I know is that he did not come here to collect water.

"We're not sure," he finally replies. Ma sighs in disappointment. "It's been like this for as long as I can remember."

"My husband is going to repair the floor," Ma says. "Among other things."

Zeke smiles darkly. "Is he really going to be back any minute, or were you just saying that because you thought I was going to hurt you?"

Emily and Ma laugh at the remark, but I don't. Zeke's smile at their reactions fades when he sees my face. "There should have been a big bucket by the pump," he says again. "I left it here last time I came."

"Strange," I say, and cross my arms. I hope he can tell that I don't believe him. The barrel of the shotgun glitters in the sun as the boy in the wide-brimmed hat shifts his weight. "Strange indeed."

"Tomorrow I'll bring my pa back with me to take a look at Hannah," he says to Ma, and she thanks him gratefully. From the front end of the cabin comes the sound of Charles yelling at Joanna, something about cheating and being rude, and Ma excuses herself to go see to them.

"I'll bring my horse with me, too," Zeke says once she's gone. "So I can carry more water."

"How often do you come to use the pump?" Emily asks. "Will we be seeing you around often, Zeke?"

His name sounds ridiculous on her tongue. I want to take a paring knife and cut it out like a growth, before the infection spreads, before it gets to her brain.

"Has your pa ever delivered a baby?" I ask, partly because I genuinely want to know and partly because I want to remind Emily what sort of things can come from flirtations and coy smiles. Has she forgotten about me?

"Don't interrupt, sister," Emily says playfully, even though I know just as well as she does that she's trying to shove my question aside. Zeke lights up even more at the sound of her giggle. "You can ask the doctor yourself tomorrow."

"Well, I used to come every day," Zeke says, ignoring me. "I liked the fresh air and exercise, truthfully. But now that there are people living here, I'll increase my load so that I only have to come a few times per week. Although, if you'd like, maybe we can arrange for me to come and tell you all some spooky stories sometime."

"I see." My sister is still smiling. "Well, I must admit that sounds like fun."

I think about the time a boy tried to win *me* over with a scary story, and all that came from it. My hand rests over my belly, and I give Zeke a dirty look. I must not allow him to hurt Emily.

"Amanda, Emily," Ma calls from the front of the cabin, and I am relieved. "I need you both now, please. Thank you for...introducing yourself, Zeke." The children peer out to inspect the stranger from behind Ma's skirts.

You're hiding something, I think as I watch the boy tip his hat to Emily with a wink. *And I won't forget it.*

"It was a pleasure, ma'am."

Zeke starts walking back toward the forest, his hand

resting on the handle of the shotgun, and Emily and I go toward the front of the cabin to help Ma. At the last minute I decide to look back. Zeke has stopped walking and is staring at the cabin. When he sees me looking, he waves. I don't return the gesture, and his hand freezes in the air.

When I look again a few minutes later, he's gone.

NINE

Seeing Zeke with Emily, how he looked at her, how she liked it, floods my mind with memories of the post boy in the mountains, and how we started out.

"You must have seen some interesting places in your travels," I said to Henry after the third or fourth time we were together. We were sprawled over the blanket, naked still from our pleasure trip, and I rested my forehead lightly against the side of his shoulder. "Tell me what it's like to be a post boy."

The forest seemed hyperactive that day. Birds chirped and squirrel feet scattered, as the creek trickled with an invigorating intensity somewhere behind us. Henry moved a piece of hair away from my face, and I decided that *this* was the way I wanted to view life forever, as a vibrant springtime earth that kept all of its darkness hidden in caves and expressed its spirit through colorful patches of flowers and fawns that wobbled determinately on their new legs.

"I might know a few tales," Henry said with a wicked grin, and curled the end of my hair with his finger. "I know a ghost story that just so happens to be real. Maybe I'll tell you for a kiss."

I giggled, intoxicated by the sunshine and his love, and pressed my lips over his with eager execution.

"That was lovely," he said after we were through, and leaned back down to face the sky. "And most definitely earned itself a spooky story."

I used to tell Joanna and Charles scary tales about the mountain, of a cloaked woman who would lure settlers away into the trees only to harvest their eyeballs for her bird, who could see the future and would whisper it into her ear. That was before they were too nervous to play with me, or tell stories with me, or let anyone watch over them besides Ma or Emily. I missed them ever so, missed being close with them.

The creature had taken that away from me.

"Amanda?" Henry said, looking at me instead of the sky now. "Are you all right, my love?"

I realized for the first time that my clenched hand was wrapped around the edge of the blanket, curled into a trembling half-fist. Dirt clung to my rigid fingertips, filled the space beneath my nails. I dropped the blanket.

"Of course," I said with a little laugh. *The devil took your soul*, I thought, *it climbed inside of you, it's never going away, it's never going away...*

I frantically wiped the dirt from my hands, then lay back down beside Henry. "I was just thinking about how much I enjoy scary stories. Please, do tell."

"Well," he started, and I was back in the embrace of springtime again. "During a recent travel run to a settlement very far away from here, an old man in the saloon told me that whenever the behavior of their children was getting out of hand, he'd tell them the legends of the local ghost."

"Is it a nasty ghost?" I smiled against the skin of his shoulder, not feeling afraid at all as his fingers moved around mine. "Those are the ones I like best. Those poor children, though. They shouldn't have to be scared into acting good."

"Isn't everybody, though?" Henry said. "I thought it was quite clever."

"Well, what did this ghost do to people? Or, I'm assuming, children, if that's who the stories were for—"

"I'll tell you about it if you let me," he laughed. "The ghost *was* the very nasty type, as it turns out. There were some tales of people going mad from it, all of which of course could be confirmed, according to the old man. One woman cut off the heads of her children and sewed them to the tops of scarecrows."

"Oh, my," I whispered. "How very dreadful."

"Yes," he agreed. "Even worse was the fact that the scarecrows came alive at night to comb the fields for food. Horses from nearby cabins went missing, and even a few children."

"Those don't sound like any ghosts I have ever heard of before," I said. "How perfectly terrifying."

"It wasn't multiple ghosts doing it, exactly," Henry explained. "It was the land itself. It had been soured by an infection of constant panic, hate and fear. The man said that in some places, the land can come out to play through the living. It can even make folks go mad."

"How hopeless," I said, then yawned as I arched my back. "And how fortunate that you were able to make the post delivery without getting your head cut off."

"That's the strangest part of all," Henry said, his voice suddenly flat. "I had to camp out a few times on my way out of the area, and each time I could have sworn I heard children giggling in the night."

"You're full of scut!" I proclaimed, nudging his leg with my knee. "No lying."

"It isn't a lie!" Henry swore. "There was something funny about that place."

"Maybe there was something funny about your brain."

"Well, that would have fit the story, all right," he said with a laugh. "Anyway, I got out of there real fast."

"No more talk of headless children." I sat up and reached for my dress. "You may walk me home now, although you won't be able to come too close, of course. If Emily sees you—"

"Apologies, my angel." Henry cut me off, his voice different than it was a few moments before. "But I don't have the time to spare. I'll be riding off once you're dressed."

I knew immediately that it was a lie. When my hands were on his naked body, he had all the time in the world.

"You didn't mention a time restraint before," I said softly, and slid the dress over my head.

"No pouting," Henry commanded. "I shall be back again when the month is half through, then again on the first of the next. Check for my signal."

"All right," I agreed with a sigh. I stood up, buttoned my dress, and shook my hair out before rebraiding it to look as neat as a pin. "Farewell then, I suppose."

"You know I cannot wait," Henry said as he hopped up, still naked, and pulled me toward him for more kisses. "And I'll be thinking about how sweet your lips taste until."

"Do you love me?" I asked, lacing my fingers together behind his back. "Like you said earlier?"

"Of course I love you." To hear him say it while I was clothed filled me with a profound sense of hope, an unexpected but welcomed result in addition to how much I enjoyed myself with him physically. Besides pleasure, Henry now also offered me hope for a future, and love, somewhere so far away from that cursed mountain. "What on earth could ever keep me away?"

TEN

Pa still isn't back by nightfall, and I become convinced that he is gone forever. I make myself sick with worry all through supper and cleanup, even though Ma doesn't seem too worried herself. She sings hymns to us from the back of the wagon as Emily and Jo and I lie in the short cut grass around the fire, her voice light and sweet and Heaven to the ears. For the first time since we arrived, I am not afraid of the snakes.

I can't remember the last time she sang to us all. It's as if her excitement about the doctor coming to inspect Hannah tomorrow has animated her back to life. What is she hoping to hear from him, exactly? While I do not know, I'm happy to have a little piece of my ma back, even if it will just be for the night.

My sisters are asleep within two songs, but I am awake long after Ma's voice fades into the night air, taking in the enormity of the starry sky while I wait for Pa's return. I lie on my back, remembering the boy with the shotgun, remembering Henry, missing Emily, when there comes a sound from somewhere in the pitch dark behind me, lacing itself into the air along with the popping embers of the fire. At first I think I'm imagining it, but as my heart continues to pound, it only gets louder.

It is the sound of an infant crying, and it is coming from inside the cabin.

The sky goes from black to a blended purple-red in a single blink, and the sound of Rocky returning with Pa, pulling the loaded wooden cart behind them, jars me awake. I sit up, confused, and look to the cabin. I can't hear the baby anymore.

I must have been dreaming.

Pa tells us that he hasn't stopped for sleep since he left yesterday morning, and he talks about the settlement as he takes Rocky's saddle off and rubs his legs down with remedy oil. The place is just where the map said it would be, Pa says, and although it was a little smaller than he imagined, the general store in town is well stocked and the owner has agreed to trade and buy homemade furniture from Pa, from wood he'll gather in the forest.

"No more furs," he says while he eats a slab of salted pork and ground wheat bread. "It'll be a nice change, steadier. Trees don't exactly hide when they see you coming. I owe them quite a few pieces for getting the flooring materials up front, of course." He takes a swig of water from his canteen. "They also told me that there was someone living in the forest."

"Yes," Ma says eagerly, watching him eat. "A young man wandered onto the property yesterday to use the well pump. He said his father is a doctor."

"What do you mean he came to use our pump?" Pa brushes a few crumbs from his beard. "Why would he need to do that?"

Ma explains how the Jacobsons have been keeping the well in working order, then tells him that the doctor is coming to inspect Hannah later today. Pa seems aggravated by the entire story.

"We mustn't start a fuss over sharing the well pump," Ma insists. "If it weren't for them, it's possible we wouldn't be able to use it by now at all. The boy said the cabin has been like this for as long as he can remember."

"I don't care what the boy had to say," Pa grumbles as he lies down on his blanket in the grass. "And having a doctor look at Hannah won't change a thing, Susan." He sets his hat over his face, ending the conversation.

I think of how relaxed Ma was last night, how light and peaceful she seemed in her songs, but that's all gone now, lost to Pa's cruel tone and the sound of the baby screaming from the wagon. I offer to wash the breakfast dishes so I don't have to bear witness to the pain in her face.

In the late morning, after he's had a chance to sleep off a little of his trip to the settlement, Pa opens the door to the cabin, untouched since our arrival, and begins walking back and forth from the well pump to splash soapy water over the blood-soaked log walls inside the cabin, to prepare them for the draw knife.

Ma cleans the inside of the window to let the sun through and encourage the flies to disperse, which they eventually do for the most part. She smashes the spider nests in the corners of the cabin with a shovel, then whisks the webbing away with a broom.

"Somebody killed an ox in there?" Charles pulls on my skirt while we watch from near the doorway. "That is disgusting!"

I wonder if I'll ever be able to erase the sight of all the blood from my mind, so much blood, more than I've ever seen in my life, even more than last winter. I take my brother's hand, and we walk together to the wagon where Joanna and Emily are sitting in the shade. Somewhere in the bed, Hannah snores softly. Emily doesn't acknowledge my presence.

"Don't worry." I smile weakly at Charles. "Pa is getting it all nice and fixed up for us."

"I heard Ma murmuring something about it when she didn't know I could hear her," Joanna says matter-of-factly and straightens the dress on the corncob doll she received for her birthday. "She said the cabin was rotted."

"She's just very stressed, Jo," Emily assures her from the top of the wagon, where she sits chewing on dried apricots. "The house isn't rotted. It was unclean, that's all. Pa will finish the floor before we know it." She pops another apricot into her mouth.

"Don't eat all of those!" Joanna whines, and reaches her little hands up to Emily. "I want some, too!"

Emily rolls her eyes, but drops a small handful of the spongy orange discs into Jo's hands anyway. "Share with Charles," she commands when she spies Joanna stuffing them all into her pocket. "They're for everybody."

She doesn't offer any to me, and I don't ask.

"When is that doctor supposed to arrive?" Pa asks again while he pours a bucket of water from the pump over his sweating head. He presses a dry cloth over his dripping beard, replaces his hat and looks toward the forest line.

"I told you already that the boy wasn't specific," Ma says. "He only said that he'd be back today with his father."

"There's a doctor coming?" Charles pipes up from where he and Joanna sit on the half-broken fence, chewing on their apricots. "Why? Is Hannah sick?"

"No, son." Pa stretches his back and looks back at the cabin in exhaustion. "Your ma just can't go on being happy with her life until a doctor tells her to, I suppose."

Shocked silence from everyone, including the children. Ma's mouth is turned down as she beats at the weeds with the rake. Why does Pa have to make it so much harder for her, always? It's as if he holds last winter against her, blames her for getting a fever and cooking away Hannah's sight and sound in the womb. It's as if he feels that she deserves to hurt over Hannah, forever.

Again, I find myself wishing that my baby sister hadn't lived through the delivery. The guilt blooms in my stomach, makes me sick, or maybe that's just real sickness from my own baby. The Lord works in mysterious ways, all right. Wish a baby dead, get another one in return as punishment. This is my reckoning.

Zeke arrives with his pa about an hour before the sun is to set, right around the time the massive sky is changing from blue to orange. They ride a fat horse with a gray body and black mane.

Ma sees him coming from the distance and begins to ready some water for them all to drink. I can see in her movements that she is still upset about Pa's words. I feel her anger in my pit and wonder if it is affecting the baby in any way. Does the little soul know that I don't want it? Can it tell?

When the Jacobsons near the cabin, Joanna and Charles scurry into the back of the wagon out of last-minute shyness. I can't help but smile at the sight of their small heads poking up from the sides to get a better look at our neighbors.

"Hello, Verners!" The man who I assume to be Doctor Jacobson calls with a friendly wave, then hops from his horse to gratefully accept a cold drink of water from Ma. He is tall and bald, with no facial hair, and a pair of wire-rimmed spectacles sits on his nose. "Thank you, my dear. It is much too hot for my taste today."

"Isn't it, though?" Ma says and fixes a misplaced curl on Hannah's forehead. "Our mountain was so much cooler, even in the middle of summer."

"I can only fantasize," the doctor says and shakes Pa's hand with a smile. "Frederick Jacobson's the name, sir, and this is my son, Ezekiel."

"Hello, Doctor," Pa says. "I appreciate you coming over to introduce yourselves and, you know...appease my wife." Beside him, Ma gazes unblinking into Hannah's face. The corner of her mouth twitches. "She's had a very hard time ever since last winter—"

"I am aware of the circumstances," Doctor Jacobson says curtly, his smile unwavering. "Zeke informed me upon his return yesterday. I am happy to inspect the child."

He steps boldly in front of Pa, causing him to take a step back. I look in surprise at Emily to gauge her reaction at the sight of our big, tough pa being intimidated by a bald man with glasses. But she isn't even listening, for all Emily can look at is Zeke.

She steps over to stand closer to the wagon, but really it's to be closer to him, and when Zeke sees me notice, I could swear his eyes narrow ever-so-slightly. The doctor peers over Ma's shoulder and at the baby.

"And this must be little Hannah," he says softly, his

mouth just a few inches away from her ear. "What a gorgeous child she is!"

"Thank you," Ma says. Behind her, Zeke says something to Emily under his breath, and she laughs into her hand. "She seems to be fine some of the time, but other times she will scream and kick for hours. It has made me wonder if perhaps she's in pain or needing something from me that I...don't understand."

Ma's voice cracks at the last word, and she clears her throat.

"The human body is a marvel," the doctor replies, his tone suddenly very serious. He cautiously slides his fat pink finger into the baby's hand. "She may seem as though she's in pain, but the fits are much more likely to be a result of her frustration. Hannah is different from most, so naturally your approach must be different, as well. You mustn't doubt yourself, for you are the mother."

I wait for Hannah to scream at the touch of a stranger. She can't even stand it when Pa or me or one of the children try to handle her, so I know the doctor is in for an earsplitting surprise. I think Ma is even more shocked than I am when Hannah tightens her grip around the finger, and reaches out to explore his arm eagerly.

"What a little sweetheart!" Doctor Jacobson exclaims, and plucks the baby from Ma's arms as if she is nothing more than a doll. "She doesn't seem to mind newcomers at all, hmm?"

Ma's jaw drops open. Pa looks irritated at his daughter's warmth, and it's easy to understand why—I don't think I've ever seen Hannah react so lovingly to him as she does Doctor Jacobson.

"Wow!" I hear Joanna say to Charles from the back of the wagon, and the doctor seems to have heard her, as well.

"What do we have here?" he calls to the wagon. "A couple of eavesdropping hideaways, hmm?"

Doctor Jacobson balances Hannah on his hip and strides over to the wagon. He shoves his free hand into his pocket, and when it comes out there are two maple candy sticks clutched inside. "If the children are hiding, whoever shall I give these sweets to?"

My brother and sister tumble out of the back of the wagon in seconds, tripping over each other as they reach eagerly for the sweets.

"Thank you, sir!" Charles says politely, and jumps up and down in excitement with Joanna. "Ma, may we eat them now? Oh, please, Ma, can't we have them?"

On the rare occasion that Pa would bring us sweets from the mountain colony, Ma would always force us to wait until after supper was eaten and cleaned up before indulging. The doctor's nature seems to have the same effect on her that it does on Hannah, though, because she offers the children a smile and nods to show that she will allow it.

The wrappers are torn off in an instant, two swift

crinkles of waxed paper followed by the sound of the children sucking eagerly at the maple sticks. Zeke and Emily wander around the yard, talking about the heat and the forest and Lord knows what else. The doctor pats the top of Charles's dark curly head before turning to the camp set up in front of our cabin.

"Sleeping outside, are you?" he asks and sets Hannah down in the clearing. He watches intently as she paws around his boots. The doctor moves his foot very carefully away to the side and observes as Hannah feels her way to follow it. "I can't imagine why anybody would choose to settle at *this* particular cabin."

"Yes, well," Pa grumbles, and shoots a glance back to the cabin. There are piles of soapsuds, pinked with blood, oozing from beneath the edges. "There was a little more work involved than I expected, but it'll be good as new before long. It's a nice, big place."

The doctor frowns at the cabin and doesn't inquire further. His face doesn't look all that different from how Zeke's did yesterday when he kept stealing glances at the window. I think about the infant cry I thought I heard in the night and shiver.

"I see," Doctor Jacobson remarks simply, and continues setting up little tests for Hannah. First he creates a small trail of pebbles that lead to a soft, fluffy rabbit's foot that has been preserved as a token, produced from his pocket. Then he stomps his foot near the first pebble to create a vibration. Hannah immediately feels around the area and finds the trail. She has the rabbit's foot in seconds, and rubs it happily over the skin on her face while she coos at the sensation.

"Remarkable!" Doctor Jacobson exclaims and adjusts the wire spectacles sliding down his nose. "Such a smart little one. In ignorance, one would assume that a child with such a condition wouldn't be able to get past the confusion enough to sort her own thoughts out, let alone follow a puzzle of pebbles. But she has adjusted seamlessly, as all of God's creatures do, I suppose."

"That's right," Pa says, looking at Ma. "That is absolutely right."

Despite the praise, Ma looks uncomfortable with Doctor Jacobson's words. "The confusion has settled a bit over time, I suppose," Ma says and bends down to rub the baby's head. "And the anger, too. Still, though, I have to admit that I've never seen her take to somebody so quickly."

The doctor looks confused by this comment. "You don't say," he says and looks into my eyes for a moment, then Pa's, as if searching for a reason as to why the baby would hate us. "Well, she's certainly a splendid child. I'd like to come check up on her progress from time to time, if you wouldn't mind."

"Of course," Ma says. "That'd be very kind of you, Doctor. Thank you."

Pa sighs. The sky has darkened several shades in the

short amount of time Doctor Jacobson has been here, and he seems to notice at the same time that I do.

"Better get back to the woods before dark," the doctor says, and replaces the hat on his bald head. "We need to get our supper started if we want to fall asleep at a decent hour, hmm, Zeke?"

Zeke nods and heads back to the horse after one more glance at Emily. "I'll see you all soon when I come for water in a few days," he says. "And don't forget that you promised to meet up for some scary stories."

"That sounds like such fun!" Charles beams through a smile that is sticky with maple. "We love scary stories."

"Thank you for the candy!" Joanna cries and hugs the doctor around his middle. "Come back any time!"

Doctor Jacobson laughs and thanks Ma again for the water. "Please, don't hesitate to call upon us if you ever need a helping hand."

"Same," Pa says and shakes the doctor's hand. "Let me know if you ever need a new piece of furniture."

"Will do," Doctor Jacobson calls over his shoulder as he mounts the gray horse with Zeke. With the click of his tongue and a quick turn, they are riding toward the woods. "See you around, neighbors!"

We watch in silence while the doctor rides away with Zeke. In a few minutes, they've disappeared into the trees, and the winds of the prairie whistle through the grasses as Ma starts to prepare supper.

"What a nice man," she remarks in an empty voice.

"I wonder what happened to his wife, the boy's mother. So sad that they only have each other now."

"I didn't like that doctor too much," Pa says. "He was rude."

"Hannah seemed to love him," Emily says. Her back is turned toward them, but I can see the suppressed half-smile bloom over her face as she tosses a few more sticks into the fire. "I think Ma's right. It's sad that they only have each other. We should invite them for supper every now and then."

"Wouldn't *that* just tickle your fancy," I murmur under my breath. Emily glares.

"I can't wait for Zeke to tell us scary stories at the fire pit." Joanna claps excitedly, and Charles follows suit. "I bet he knows some really good ones."

"Just as long as it's nothing satanic," Ma says, and Pa agrees.

When dinner has passed and it's time to go to bed, I pray to God that I don't dream of the crying baby inside the cabin again. *Just give my heart a rest, please.* I toss and turn nervously until I fall asleep in an obscure position, with my arms resting above my head and my fingertips grazing the dirt of the prairie.

In the dead of night, when I feel a tiny hand wrap itself around my wrist, I refuse to open my eyes. *It's only a piece of grass in the breeze*, I lie to myself, still half asleep. *There is nothing wrong here. There is nothing wrong with me.*

ELEVEN

"What between two sisters can stay bitter for this long?" Ma wonders aloud suddenly one afternoon, after Hannah has fallen asleep in the wagon. "'And be ye kind to one another, tenderhearted, forgiving one another, even as God for Christ's sake hath forgiven you.' That is from the book of Ephesians, Amanda."

I continue to rake the dirt of any rocks or dead grass or weeds, shoving it all outside the clearing of the newly maintained yard. In just a week we've managed to get rid of all the weeds, and four days ago Pa took a break from rebuilding the floor of the cabin to repair and complete the fence. I haven't been inside the cabin since our arrival, but I can say with confidence that at least the yard looks much better.

Forgiving one another, I think and bend down painfully to uproot an especially stubborn stone with my hands. *If only she knew just how much of a sinner I really am.* Talk of forgiveness wouldn't flow from her mouth with such warmth. It certainly hasn't flown from Emily's.

"There is no quarrel," I answer simply and finish with the rake. My body feels strained, too strained almost, and I wonder at what point I won't be able to do hard labor anymore. What if that moment comes before Ma and Pa notice my belly? I'd have to tell them then, actually physically say the words *I am with child*. The idea causes the back of my neck to break out into even more of a sweat.

I make my way to the pile of smooth, round stones that sit before the front door. Ma's had the children collecting them for days, rewarding them with sugar lumps from the supply pile to encourage them to make haste. Today is finally the day when enough stones have been gathered, and now that we've finished preparing the clearing, we can begin to line the area with them.

Emily is a ways beyond the clearing, playing tag with Joanna and Charles and keeping them busy while we work.

"I will pretend that I don't know you are lying to me," Ma remarks and goes over to check on the baby. After she's confirmed that Hannah is still sleeping, she motions for me to bring the rocks over to her.

"No lies, Ma."

I kneel and gather the stones in my skirt, then walk over to her and carefully allow them to spill over the freshly raked soil at her feet. We crouch side by side and begin lining the raked portion of the clearing with the stones. After the line is no more than five feet long, Hannah stirs in the back of the wagon and begins to yell.

"Drat," Ma mutters under her breath. "I was hoping to get much more of this done today."

There is something that I need to do. After seeing Doctor Jacobson win Hannah over so effortlessly, using the *she only likes Ma* excuse to make myself feel better about standing by and doing nothing is no longer an option for me. If I'm being forced to grow up, I might as well start somewhere.

"I'll watch her, Ma," I offer, and stand to brush the dirt from my knees. "You go ahead and keep working."

It is the first time anyone in the family has offered to help directly with Hannah, and the shock is evident in Ma's face. She looks up at me admiringly, as though I am an angel, as though I am only acting from the pure goodness of my own heart.

My revelation makes me feel despicable. Perhaps if I had just grown up after last winter, if I had used it to make myself a stronger woman, I would have laughed in the post boy's face when he asked me where I lived. I would have been a good sister to Hannah from the start.

"Are you sure?" Ma asks, clearly doubtful as she gazes over at the wagon again. "She's awfully difficult to handle for anyone besides me."

"I'm her big sister, Ma," I reason, except in my head

I'm saying *I'm going to have my own baby, Ma.* "I should be able to take care of her for you once in a while."

"Well, thank you, Amanda." She breaks into a smile, a real one, and it only makes me feel worse. "The Lord has blessed me with a selfless daughter."

I don't bother to correct her, for her smile is too beautiful, and soon I won't be seeing it for a long, long time. I remove Hannah from the wagon, and she instantly knows that I'm not Ma, which causes her to thrash and scream, her warbled pitch even louder and harder than usual.

Ma looks up from the line of stones nervously, but I insist that everything is just fine and bring the baby with me to a spot in the clearing that is shaded by the cabin.

I sit cross-legged on the dirt and cut grass and try to press the baby's head to my neck, like Ma does, but Hannah is still struggling against me, thrashing and wailing and throwing her skull from side to side with remarkable force. The side of her head collides with my jaw, and it makes her cry out all the more.

"Hush, sweetness," I whisper, even though I know she cannot hear me. This is the longest I have ever held my sister.

I force her wriggling body against mine despite the screams, and begin to take breaths that are loud and long and slow.

"Huuuuuuuuh," I hum as I exhale. My chest vi-

brates with the sound, and I know Hannah can feel it. *"Huuuuuuuuuuuh."*

For a few seconds, nothing happens. After the fourth exhale, the baby stops struggling and falls limp in my arms, all of her weight suddenly pressed against me, and for a moment I think she has gone to sleep. Ma looks up from her work in amazement. I turn my head to observe Hannah's face and am shocked to see that her ever-still eyes are wide-open.

"Huuuuuuuuuh," I hum again, and the baby's hand begins to move over my face like a curious sea star.

She touches my lips, my nose, my eyes, devouring them, learning every curve. She pulls at my hair, then runs her hand gently over it, squeezing the different sections of my braid in between her tiny, curious fingers. As she feels, her little face twists into a variety of expressions, some cute, some atrocious, all of them bright and quick as a flash before fading into the next.

"Baaargh," Hannah moans along with me as I exhale.

I run my fingers through the baby's curls as I continue breathing aloud. Hannah gurgles at the softened touch, and goose bumps flourish over her little arms.

I hold her like that, rocking and humming and running my hands over her head, until Ma finishes lining the yard. After a while, I lay the baby on her back in the warm dirt. She starts to panic at first, but I quickly slide my hands down her legs and put her bare feet up against my chest as I continue to hum. Hannah breaks into a smile that warms my blood, and I am suddenly overcome with the urge to sob.

For months I've had horrible thoughts about this baby, I've been sure that my *life* was horrible, I've been unable to imagine a future to be desired. But in Hannah's brief smile, I now see endless possibilities, possibilities that are already ruined because of what I've gone and done, possibilities that don't include raising a child completely alone.

I watch Hannah for the remainder of the afternoon. The rest of the family looks on in dumb confusion, but Ma seems lighter, happier, as though I have lifted an invisible weight from her shoulders. Already her posture has improved, and her face is much more relaxed.

Just before Ma and Emily are about to start on supper, Pa emerges from the cabin and announces that he has finished the floor.

"You're sure it's ready to live in?" I ask while Hannah tugs at my hair. Something inside of me feels hesitant to go inside.

"It's ready," Pa says. "I told my family I would provide them with a home, and I have done it. Everybody come see. We'll eat supper and sleep inside tonight!"

We all head for the door with slow, hesitant steps, and I suddenly remember the crying infant and the tiny hand wrapped around my wrist in the night. Why am I filled with such dread at the idea of sleeping inside? Camping has been horrible, but it's been so long since we left the mountain that I'm almost used to it by now. With a final sigh that causes Hannah's smile to fade, I walk inside.

Pa has lit five oil lamps, one for each corner of the large room with another hanging from a thick wire hook that protrudes from the roof. All of the bloodied bark has been scraped off with Pa's draw knife, and fresh clay has been slathered in between the logs. The new floor looks wonderful, and as impossible as I would have thought this to be when we first arrived, it smells wonderful, too—woodsy and fresh, clean, like a true new start.

"Oh, Edmund." Ma gasps softly and rests her hand on her chest. "It's beautiful, absolutely *beautiful*. There is so much space!"

This is the warmest I've seen her act toward Pa since before we left the mountain. He seems to notice it, too, and kisses the top of her head, a proud grin awakening on his face. Ma's happy mood continues while we empty the wagon and arrange our things in the cabin, and she gives Hannah big kisses on the nose after every time another section is organized and complete.

The new cabin is able to fit all of the tools from our old woodshed—the draw knife, the grinding stone for sharpening blades, the augurs used to drill holes in wood. Besides the scattered array from the shed, this home also allows us to store all of our cooking pots and utensils inside, instead of keeping them tucked in a cluster right outside the front door.

The size of the fireplace matches the space around it. Even with the iron frame used to hold pots over the flame placed inside, there is enough room for Charles to walk around in it if he crouches. He and Joanna dart in and out of its mouth, making faces at each other around the sides of the empty stew pot in the center.

The rocking chair looks lonely in the middle of the huge room. Both mattresses are arranged in their own corners, each with more than enough space to easily store our individual piles of clothing against the wall while still leaving plenty of walking room. Pa promises that it won't feel so empty once he's built a shelf, a headboard, and a table with some chairs.

"It's ready for the final touch!" Ma claps excitedly once everything is in place. She pulls a large brown furry thing from the corner with the woodshed tools, tied tight into a wide roll with cloth strips, and Pa grins from ear to ear at the sight of it.

"Old Griz!" he says affectionately to the hairy pile as Ma unties the strips. "I was wondering when you were going to come out to play."

She rolls out the grizzly-bear rug that Pa made for her when they were young, his first bear killed on a hunt and a permanent member of the Verner family ever since. The massive head clunks over the hollowed floor like a rock, and the claws scrape lightly across the hardwood while Ma adjusts the rug's position.

Because of all the fuss, dinner consists of dried meat, dried fruit and nuts. The children sit in a circle on the floor with Emily while I play a tickling game with Hannah, who is more than happy to notice that I no longer hesitate to touch her or be within reach of her chubby little hands.

"I can't even hold her like you are, Amanda," Pa admits from where he sits in the floor, cleaning his rifle. "It's like you've put her under some sort of spell!"

"There will be no mention of spells or black magick in this home," Ma says as she rocks before the glowing fireplace, her Bible in her lap. "This is a home of the Lord, and we will treat it as such."

"Oh, you know what I meant." Pa sighs and peers into the barrel of the gun. "I'm just impressed is all. Amanda sure has a way with our Hannah."

This is the first time that Pa has spoken to me with tenderness in his voice for nearly a year. It fills me with a joy that I didn't know I wanted, a sort of cozy familiarity that I didn't realize I was missing.

"It comes naturally to you, certainly," Emily says, her voice flat. She rips a piece of dried meat with her front teeth. "You seem to have a gift with babies."

I shoot her a look. She raises an eyebrow at me and takes another bite. Perhaps she is still grouchy over the absence of Zeke. He hasn't come once for water like he promised he would, and I can't help but feel a very sick satisfaction over it. If she's going to continue treating me like an acquaintance, I don't want her to have anyone else to be close with either. Let her see what it's like to be alone, let her be the one pushed to the realization that she and I need each other.

"Well, it doesn't surprise me that Hannah has taken so well to Amanda." Ma smiles at me from the rocking chair. "You are sixteen after all, and by God's grace becoming more and more of a woman every day."

Hannah squeals in glee as I clap her hands together, but my stomach turns. I know what's coming next, and as much as I wish to stop it I know what Ma is about to say.

"Someday sooner than you think, you may find yourself married with your own family to take care of in such a loving manner."

I start to rest my hand over my stomach when I jump at the sound of someone knocking on the glass window from the outside—*tap tap tap!* I look to the window in alarm, only to see nobody.

"What is it, daughter?" Ma asks.

"Didn't anybody hear that?" I say. "Someone knocked on the window."

Emily tries to hide her excitement, but I see right through the attempt. "Perhaps it's the Jacobson boy coming for his water?"

The Jacobson boy? Does she really think she sounds less

giddy than if she had called him Zeke? And if he hasn't come to collect any water until now, I have a feeling that our well pump isn't the only resource they have. Still, it is odd that he came in the night.

Pa looks up from his rifle. "Really?" he says. "I think I missed it." He stands and disappears outside. We all sit by in silence, listening to Pa call out *hello?* into the dark prairie, waiting for someone to answer him. The sound of his footsteps moves in a slow circle around the cabin, and before long I see the top of his head flick by the window. He comes back in and shuts the door behind him.

"You imagined it, daughter," Pa says, a touch aggravated at being pulled away from his gun. "I knew I didn't hear anything."

"I *did* hear it," I say fiercely, irritated that nobody else heard it and nervous as to who exactly is out there knocking on windows at night. "I did."

"Nothing to cause a fuss over," Ma croons from her chair. "Mistakes happen. Our lives are going on just fine."

"It wasn't a mistake—"

"Amanda." Pa raises his voice as he looks at me from across the cabin. The tenderness he had for me a moment ago is gone. The light of the oil lamp causes his beard to cast a ghostly shadow over the rest of his face. "There wasn't anybody there. Or if there was, they sure ran off in a heartbeat."

I imagine Zeke Jacobson tearing through the dark prairie, with only the light of the moon to guide him back to the forest. What would he do once he reached the trees? The moon wouldn't help guide him through those.

When everybody is finished eating, Ma strokes Emily's freshly brushed hair while she reads through the book of Ephesians in a silky voice. She reads over the verse she quoted to me earlier today, the one about forgiveness, and slows her tone to emphasize the words as she speaks them.

If Emily absorbs the message, she doesn't show any signs. She's probably mad at me for making her think that Zeke was here. She probably thinks that I did it on purpose to torture her, that I'm so miserable I can't stand the idea of her being happy, that just because I ruined my own life I'm somehow expecting her to take away some of the pain, whether it is her responsibility to or not. That is the kind of person my sister thinks I am.

"I'm going to fall asleep early," I say and change into my nightshirt after Pa goes outside to smoke tobacco from his pipe. "I'm exhausted."

"I'm sorry, dear." Ma stops reading and places her finger on the page so she can look up. "Was the baby too much for you today?"

"Oh, no," I insist. "I enjoyed it, really. It was just a big day is all, with moving everything into the cabin."

Ma thanks me for what seems like the hundredth

time and begins reading again. I pause before crawling beneath the thick quilt on our old mattress, savoring the fact that at least I will no longer be sleeping on the ground. It was bad for the baby, I'm sure of it. The bed is more wonderful than I remember, and I exhale deeply as I close my eyes and turn to face the wall. My body sinks into the soft mattress, cradled, and I want to stay in bed forever.

Phantom sounds aside, the first night in my new home feels admittedly more comfortable than I ever could have hoped. No more worrying about snakes, no more pretending to ignore the stagnant presence of a blood-soaked cabin.

Mistakes happen, like Ma said, and once my big one is brought into the light, our lives will continue to go on, right? Why couldn't they? I will repent for my sins, I will use this to become stronger, I am changed. Maybe tomorrow I can try to talk to Emily, fix things between us.

Maybe tomorrow my fresh start can *really* begin.

TWELVE

The pain strikes me with an intensity that almost causes me to scream into the night. It is below my belly, deep inside of me, and feels like a knife cutting through all my muscle and gristle like they are nothing but butter left out in the sun. I throw my hand over my mouth to conceal the gasp, stand and stumble to the door, slipping out carefully as to not make a sound.

The dark sky of the prairie is streaked with early morning dim blues and yellows, something that would usually take my breath away with its beauty, but I hardly notice it now as I try to get as far away from the cabin as possible so I can howl into the back of my sleeve without waking anyone. I run for what feels like miles through pebbles and grass and flowered weeds before I collapse in another wave of pain.

I feel a terrible rush of wetness and grab beneath my nightshirt, in between my legs. My hand comes back covered in blood, thick and rich and disgustingly fragrant in the cool morning air. Even as the tears pour down my hot face and I stifle another scream with my clean hand, I know what has happened.

You got what you prayed for.

I sob into my skirt, holding my shaking and bloodied hand as far away from me as I can.

No, no, no.

With each wave of searing pain I see Henry's face. How it studied mine with such curiosity the first time we met, when I came to the mountain town with my pa. How it twisted in pleasure while he rode me in the woods behind our cabin with animalistic urgency. How it gazed upon me in disgust when I told him I carried his child.

The agony continues longer than I could have ever imagined. I hear someone behind me before I see them. In my delirium of pain I assume it's Ma or Pa, come to find me out and bash my head in as punishment. When it's Emily who sinks beside me and pulls my head into her chest all I can think is, *at least there's that.* Then I hear my own screams and mistake them for my baby's and pray that I die anyway.

I sit with my sister, wailing into her lap, while she rocks me back and forth, and my baby gushes from my body and soaks into the earth.

THIRTEEN

When the bleeding finally stops, the sun is dangerously close to peeking up and over the horizon of the flatlands. My sister knows that we have very little time.

"We need to move," she whispers into my hair, after my cries have died away. "I'm so sorry, Amanda, but we need to move now."

So I frantically rub my hand, still coated in the terrible crimson, against a slew of dried grasses before wiping away the excess muck on a clean spot of my nightshirt. After hiding the blood-soaked shirt underneath a divot in the earth that is covered by dense growths of waist-length grass, Emily asks me if I'm all right.

"I do not know," I say in a shaking voice as I stand naked before her. The insides of my thighs are still smeared with the heavy blood. "My baby is dead, Emily."

"Yes," she says and puts her hand on my shoulder. I wish she'd say more on the matter. "I need to get you some clean clothes while you wash yourself at the pump, before they wake up."

My shock makes the world feel unfamiliar and new. I wish she'd tell me if this was a good thing or a bad thing, if God did this on purpose, if he suddenly realized *Oh, my, well, isn't* this *a big mess for poor Amanda Verner,* or if it was even God that did it at all. I want her to tell me if this terror was carefully thought-out and written into my plan, or if I'm some sort of error of the Lord's nature that has broken through the barrier and spiraled straight into Satan's claws.

You prayed *for this.*

The blood drying on my legs is unclean, excess sin that stinks of a much different future than what I've prepared myself for in the past months. Still, I feel heavier instead of lighter, and sick with lingering cramps as we walk back to the cabin in silence. Emily wraps her arms around my shoulders so I can lean on her as we make our way to the well pump.

"Wait here," she whispers when we get close. She disappears around the corner of the cabin to go inside.

Once she's returned, Emily helps me finish splashing water from the pump over myself. It runs red over my calves and feet, then pink, then clear. The water is shockingly cold, but I don't allow myself to flinch. *You deserve much worse than cold water.*

Ma and Pa awaken only minutes after I wiggle into

the clean underwear, skirt and blouse that Emily fetched me.

"What are you two doing up already?" Ma's voice calls from outside the front end of the cabin. "Is everything all right?"

"Everything's fine, Ma," Emily bellows back from where we stand near the pump, as she scours me from head to toe for any signs that might have been left over. "Amanda felt slightly overheated this morning. She just needed a moment to splash some water on her face."

"Amanda?" Pa barks from inside the cabin, his voice smoky and hoarse in the early hour. "Is that true?"

"I'm feeling better," I say with as much enthusiasm as I can manage, but my voice sounds fragile, danger-ously close to breaking. Luckily, neither of them take further notice. When we go back inside, Ma calls for Emily to help her with breakfast and hands Hannah to me so she can fetch some water for the oatmeal. She just plops the baby onto my hip, like it's nothing, and turns away. Hannah smiles and grabs on to my braid.

Suddenly my knees are shaking and feel as though they are about to give out, and I sway with the baby's added weight. I hear Ma outside, using the pump, stand-ing in remnants of her own grandchild, and I have to sit down with Hannah on the spot to keep from faint-ing. My baby sister clings to me, all but asking for me to return the affection, but I just look down at her as the world descends into madness around me.

My heart feels cold.

I don't tickle her, or kiss her neck, or hum against her body, and I suspect it's the reason her tiny hands act mopey and confused as they rake over the wooden floor to feel around for Joanna and Charles's jacks. She periodically reaches out to grab my leg, to make sure that I'm still here, but I can hardly bring myself to do anything more than give her a weak nudge in assurance. Her dark little eyebrows furrow around her still, gray eyes.

Emily watches me very closely throughout breakfast and cleanup. When I go to wash the oatmeal pot outside, she puts her hand on mine to stop me.

"We can trade days," she offers with a weak smile. At least it's a smile, and at least it's for me. "You just sit and take in the morning, sister."

It almost sickens me that I had to miscarry my baby for her to offer me smiles and kindness again, but I don't have the mental or physical energy to become bitter over it now. More than ever, I need my best friend. Without another word, Emily and I hug each other tightly.

"I'm here for you, sister," she whispers. "And I am so sorry."

I knew ever since I was seven years old that Emily was meant to be the big sister, and I was meant to be the little one, following and pestering and making things difficult when really they were quite simple. God must have mistaken our souls for one another, sent them to the wrong bodies. An understandable mistake, since certain pieces of us might as well be one of the same.

"They never have to know," Emily murmurs, and she uses my shoulder to soak up a tear that has run down her cheek. "I'm certain the Lord would understand."

"All right."

I haven't cared if the Lord understood me since last winter.

"I see you two have finally made up." Ma beams from the doorway. "It's about time. Nothing in this world is powerful enough to tear two sisters apart."

Neither Emily nor I bother to correct her.

Everybody seems eager to spend some time out of the sun and inside the cabin, and I find myself grateful beyond words that the room is large enough for everybody to live comfortably and spread out with their own amount of personal space. If I had to endure this torture in the tiny mountain cabin, I would have lost my mind again, without a doubt.

The children immerse themselves with their newly unpacked playthings in one corner, while Ma reads from the Bible and Pa gets geared up to go into the forest for some wood. I sit pretending to draw, my back against the hard rough wall of the logs, and Emily eyes me from where she goes through her button collection nearby. *Thank you for giving me space without making me ask for it*, I want to say.

"I'm going to take Rocky and the cart so I can load up a bunch at once," Pa says before stepping out into the sun. His rifle lies across his back, and deerskin gloves peek out from the top of his breeches. He places his hat over his head and looks back at us all, sitting comfortably in the home that he made for us. His face is lit up with pride. "I'll see you all in a few hours."

Once Hannah wakes up I avoid her altogether, and pretend that I need to relieve myself when she reaches away from Ma and starts to wail and search for me. I can hear her cries from where I lean against the back of the empty wagon outside, low pitched and warbled and ugly, and I feel as though I would do *anything* to silence her. My fingers curl into my palms until the nails create crescent-shaped slashes, stinging with blood, and I clench my teeth until I fear they will crack.

I hardly make it to bedtime without screaming.

Then, in the night, I hear the sound of the crying infant again, right outside the end of the cabin, around where the well pump is. I'm still groggy from sleep, and something in my head tells me that it's my baby crying for me, that I have to get to it, but once I stand up and awaken a bit more I realize that it isn't possible, that my baby died early this morning and there shouldn't be any sound outside the cabin at all.

Yet the crying carries on, loud enough to wake everybody up, and my family continues to sleep as though it isn't happening. I refuse to accept that the Lord would mock me in such a way. I walk outside and around the corner of the cabin, stubborn and sure, the moonbeams casting a silver glow over the prairie. With each step I challenge the sound of the crying to carry on.

There's no way that I am going to see a baby lying on the bloodied ground beneath the pump when I turn the corner. It simply isn't possible. Yet the sound continues, growing louder as I approach the back of the cabin. I continue holding my breath, even though my chest is beginning to hurt, and step into the back clearing.

The crying stops instantly. As if to confirm my victory, I walk up to the well pump and rest my hand on it. There's nothing out here; like I suspected, there are only the sounds of my mind. But why have I heard the cries twice now, once before I lost my baby, and once after?

It's like a follow-up to a warning I never understood. Did my mind know the miscarriage was coming somehow, somewhere deep down in the subconscious? Was it trying to warn me beforehand? I go to turn back for the cabin, but something catches my eye in the distance, a tiny flash of metallic green light in the shadows.

Up ahead, right around the spot where Emily found me collapsed in the dirt, I can see the piercing reflected shine of what looks like a pair of animal eyes peering at me through the darkness. They are so low to the ground that they can't belong to a coyote, but are large and still enough not to be a jackrabbit's. I strain my eyes, willing the moon to help me make out the creature, and slowly but surely a shape comes into view. I freeze, suddenly terrified that I am out here alone, suddenly understanding why I will never come out at night again.

The eyes belong to a baby. A baby, standing upright in the grass, staring at me without a motion or a sound. My spine feels alive, like there are ants crawling over it deep beneath the muscle, and my breath catches in my throat.

The baby still hasn't moved by the time I start walking, backward, toward the front of the cabin. Even after the figure fades from my view into the shadows, I don't turn my back in fear that it will get me. Once the front door is in sight, I bolt for it.

I climb back into bed, my blood uneasy and my heart pounding in my ears, and that's when the crying starts up again, just outside the wall near the well pump. Nobody stirs, and this time I am not surprised. They are not the ones being haunted.

Haunted.

I am being haunted by the ghost of my unborn child.

FOURTEEN

Hannah was blue when she was born. Emily, Joanna and Charles had all been a grayish pink color, but when Hannah tore her way into this world I knew instantly that something was very wrong. There was no weak or startled cry from the still, blue baby, just a horrible wet slapping sound as she slipped out, feet first, from Ma's torn womanhood and into Pa's arms.

There was no midwife, like there had been for all my other siblings and myself. The snow had been too deep to reach the village on the other side of the mountain for close to four months straight, and our tiny home in the sky was transformed into an icy prison.

By then, we were all a little strange.

When the baby finally came out, Ma's guttural howls were silenced for the first time in hours.

Emily covered her mouth and began to cry at the sight of Hannah. I stood in dumb shock, still holding Ma's right leg up in a sort of daze. How long had it been?

It felt like years since the labor had started, and I had no inkling if it was early or late. Ma's face and hair were soaked with perspiration. There was a heavy stink in the air.

"Please, Lord," Pa begged under his breath, hitting the slimy, blue baby on the back with one hand while Emily and I watched. *"Please*, Lord."

Once Ma had gotten the illness four months earlier, it wouldn't stop for anything, not desperate prayers, not a pregnancy and certainly not a snowstorm that kept us stranded without any help or extra supplies. Nobody else ever caught it; Pa said it was because her body was especially prone when with child.

"Amanda," Pa snapped, accusatory, as if he could sense that I hated Hannah already for what she'd done to my mother. "Help me."

I gently set Ma's trembling leg down on the bed, the sheets and mattress clotted with blood and birth fluid and stinking waste. Joanna and Charles were still sitting in the opposite corner of our family's log cabin, facing the wall and playing a game of jacks with each other like we'd told them to do when things started looking bad. They never turned, as commanded. They had no idea what was behind them. And at six and five, they shouldn't have had to know.

I only just got to Pa when Hannah started moving. Her tiny arms and legs flailed around like those of an overturned mountain beetle. She took sharp, violent little breaths for a few moments, and her color warmed a shade. She wasn't crying.

"Is my baby all right?" Ma slurred from the soaking bed as Emily wiped her face. "What's happening?"

"I think she's all right," Pa said, his voice deep and breaking apart under the stress, and that's how Ma found out the baby was a girl.

But I could see Pa's face as he looked down at Hannah, whose eyelids were pulled into half-open slits as she took in those noisy little breaths. Soon, the breaths turned into weak, off-key yelps. She pawed at his hands as if fighting them away.

Pa sliced the cord away from her navel with his knife, and I wondered if I would vomit before the night was through. Emily whimpered.

"Why isn't she crying?" Ma demanded again.

I went to her side and felt her face. Still hot, searingly hot, just as it had been for hours now and for most of this winter. I wondered if Ma would ever be able to remember anything from the past four months, if she didn't end up dying first.

"She's perfectly fine, Ma," I whispered gently, and Emily looked at me in shock. *Hush*, I wanted to say.

I motioned for Emily to help me clean up the bed and the area around it. We gathered the excess blankets, heavy with thickened blood, and shoved them through the freezing window, little by little, out into the snow. As

I pulled the crudely cut glass panel back in, I could have sworn I heard someone call my name from outside.

Pa had warned us that our minds might turn funny from being trapped in here all together for so long. I needed to ignore it.

Without a word, I swiped the large tin cooking pot from the corner of the cabin and made my way to the front door. The door was still mostly jammed shut, but after beating at it for a few minutes I was able to create an opening just wide enough to scoop some snow into the pot. After wrestling the door shut again, I set the pot over the fire and waited as its contents melted away.

There is nobody outside, I thought. *I didn't hear a thing.*

Joanna and Charles had both placed their hands over their ears by now. Hannah's yelps continued, growing louder by the minute. None of my other siblings had sounded like this. Wasn't it supposed to be a small bout of crying followed by calm and quiet? Or was I misremembering?

Emily was waiting for me and the pot of hot water at the bedside, with a small pile of clothing and linen scraps in her arms. They were the last clean ones, set aside especially for the birth weeks beforehand, and we would need to use them well.

Nobody asked about Hannah. We were too scared to. Instead, Emily and I silently dunked the fabric pieces into the water and began to clean Ma's body of all the blood and fluids.

Pa used one of the scraps to clean Hannah off properly, then wrapped her in the many layers of cotton and wool that Emily and I had gathered when Ma's labor started. I held the gasping baby for a moment while Pa went over to Ma.

Hannah's eyes were a stunning but strange gray color, and I wondered even then why they weren't moving to look into mine. Despite her tiny size, her cheeks were soft and puffy, and she had several thick wisps of dark hair that curled around the top and sides of her face.

"Hello, baby," I whispered into her ear to try and calm her, but the attempt to soothe only failed. Hannah clawed at my face, grabbed at my hair, made horrible yelling sounds. The amount of strength she had for what she had just gone through astounded me. Even healthy babies were slow and weak at first.

The thought occurred to me that perhaps Ma's fever had spawned a demon.

Pa pulled a newly cleaned Ma up and propped her against the headboard. Her breaths were long and steady, and he announced that the fever was finally starting to go down, thank the Lord. Pa wriggled her soaking nightshirt up around her shoulders and took Hannah back from me. The baby fed eagerly while Ma talked nonsense in her sleep. While Hannah nourished herself, Pa pulled the nightshirt off around the top of Ma's head and replaced it with a clean one from Emily.

Outside, the snow was still never-ending, causing

the cabin to take on a dull, blue tone, which only made Hannah's color look all the worse. The air was frigid. Emily and I dumped the bloody water out the window and immediately began working on relighting the fire. Pa hummed an old hymn in his deep voice, and told Joanna and Charles to come meet their new baby sister.

The children approached the bed with slow caution, the fear all too evident in their large brown eyes and flushed skin.

"Is she all right, Pa?" Charles asked in a weak voice. My brother looked around the bed with wide eyes, at the blood on the floor and the soiled rags piled nearby, before turning to the baby.

"The Lord spared the lives of both Hannah and your ma," Pa said firmly. "And that is the greatest gift we could ever ask for. Everything is fine."

"But her eyes—" Joanna broke her silence for the first time in hours. She leaned closer to the baby with a twisted face. "I think there's something wrong with them!"

The back of Pa's hand flew into Joanna's face with such a swift and sudden force that all of us jumped. He had never hit one of us before, had never even come close. The sound of the baby suckling on Ma became deafening, nearly unbearable.

"There is *nothing* wrong with her," Pa snapped, his voice rising. "This is your kin, do you understand me? This is your baby sister from God."

Poor little Jo's hand flew to her cheek, where an angry red mark was already beginning to bloom. Her lips failed to hold the barrier and quick, pitiful sobs began to escape. Pa raised his hand again, as if daring her to continue. Joanna fell silent.

The snow is eating away at us, I thought. *It is turning our hearts into ice.*

"Everybody get some sleep while you can," Pa said, breaking the silence, and went to lie down next to Ma and Hannah, who were both still. They looked like corpses, tinged strange colors, positioned like grotesque dolls over each other on the bed. Pa checked to make sure they were both breathing, and everybody lay down.

The baby started crying again within the hour, and she didn't stop for a long, long time. Was it three days? Four? Six? However long it was, it felt like years.

Years of only opening my eyes when Pa commanded me to move out of the way so that he could get one thing or the other for Ma or the baby, or when my assistance was needed to turn over the mattress or re-cover it with a crudely washed sheet. The children cried on and off over the deafening sound of the baby, and Emily rebraided her hair dozens of times a day to keep her fingers busy and her eyes downward. Pa stuffed strips of cloth into his ears.

Hannah kept screaming.

Ma kept coughing.

The walls of the cabin began to move inward, making the space even smaller, taking more air away, suffocating us all, slowly, slowly.

For the first time, I prayed that the baby had not survived the delivery.

Why us?

Pa begged the Lord for mercy.

How cruel.

Ma's cough kept on.

The walls moved in closer.

For the first time, I wondered if God was real.

Once the tiny cabin was finally still and quiet, I arose in the dim light of what could have been either early morning or evening, and went to stand in front of the window once again. Everybody in the family was sleeping heavily, or perhaps they were dead; I neither knew nor cared as I stepped over their bodies and made my way to the tiny square of glass that mocked me with the promise of outside.

All I wanted was to look out into the open space of the earth and remind myself that freedom was still awaiting me, that the world included much more than the inside of this matchbox, that I hadn't died and gone to Hell. After wiping the condensation from the freezing window with the sleeve of my dress, I leaned close enough for the glass to touch the tip of my nose.

And that is when I saw the devil.

It was the strangest thing, but I swear he *heard* me

looking at him from all the way across the forest, through the trees and trees and trees that seemed to go on forever, surrounding me, smothering me, trapping me there on that mountain.

I saw him and he knew, he *heard*, he stopped dead in his prowl and cocked his head toward me with a viciousness that caused me to jump. I squinted through the glass, unable to believe what I was seeing, and wondered if I was dying and if he had come into this hellish storm just to collect me.

While the creature stood peering at me, motionless now, his lips parted to reveal gnarled black fangs, and I could hear his whisper as if he was standing right next to me.

"Sinner."

Then he was coming for me, all black and shining with horns and claws and those gleaming gnarled fangs. He stepped through the falling snowflakes, leaving steaming footsteps of blood that bloomed into the ice.

"I've come to devour your soul," the whisper inside my ear said, and I began to scream. His voice wavered like notes played on a fiddle, it sounded familiar, it sounded like *mine*.

I fell back from the window, still screaming, throwing my hands in front of me to keep the creature away, while my family cried out in confusion from their beds.

I only remember little bits for a while after that—the

silence, the crying, the scratches I kept reopening on my face and arms with my fingernails. I don't remember when Ma got better, or when she started reading to me from the Bible every night until the snow melted, or when Emily went anywhere except by my side with her hand in mine.

I do remember hearing them argue about me. Ma blamed herself for Hannah, and for me, as well. Pa was angry that she wasn't more thankful for the baby's life, or her own, for that matter. He told her over and over again that it was the isolation that had turned me strange, that as soon as the spring came everything would straighten out. *It was a miracle the entire family survived at all*, he bellowed. *Amanda will get better soon.*

When my tongue found itself capable of allowing me to speak once again, I told Emily that I didn't know what I saw out the window that had set me off. I kept it from her until after we were out, after it was spring and the snow was only slush gathered around the bottom of the tree trunks and the sounds of animals could be heard once again in the air of the mountain. I told her then, but only because I couldn't lie about it anymore.

I couldn't pretend that I hadn't seen him, calling for me, wanting to eat my soul, for every time I heard a snapping branch or scatter of animal feet in the forest, I was certain he had returned for me, his sinner.

Your mind wasn't right, Emily pleaded with me, finally understanding my ever-wide eyes and jumpy demeanor. *You should have told me, sister. No more lies. You should have let me protect you and tell you that it wasn't real. The winter made you strange. Your mind made a mistake, that's all.*

No.

There are no mistakes, no matter how cruel. There is only God's plan, sung over and over again like some lovely children's rhyme told on rainy days. *Smitten lies and bloody thighs and a prairie home reeking of evil!*

What is happening on this prairie? Is there evil within it, like the place in Henry's story, torturing me from afar until the time comes to claim its prey? Is my whole family doomed to death after all?

Or is it, *all* of it...just...me?

FIFTEEN

The morning after I see the baby standing amidst the tall grass, I wake up with a tearstained face and a dull but engulfing headache. I tell Ma that I'm ill and need to rest through breakfast, and after checking my temperature with a concerned face, she sighs in relief at the absence of a fever.

"You have such dark circles under your eyes, Amanda," Ma says, while Emily looks on from where she is lacing up her boots. "Have you been sleeping all right? You're not too used to lying on the ground now, are you?"

"No, Ma," I croak, keeping my eyes closed. "The mattress is wonderful. I just need a little bit more sleep, that's all."

But I don't sleep. I lie in bed, under the quilt even though it's late enough in the morning for the heat to be stifling again, and sweat myself into the sheets and feathers while I listen to the sound of the children arguing over a toy and Emily making breakfast and Ma comforting an especially irritable Hannah.

After they've finished eating, Pa goes outside to work on the table set he's been carving up, and the children follow. I hear Joanna ask Emily if I might feel like playing tag when I wake up, and Emily says she doesn't know. Soon I hear them screaming and whooping from outside, and I know that I'm finally alone.

A hand takes my wrist and squeezes. I snap upright in bed with a scream, only to startle Emily enough to drain all the color from her face.

"It's just me!" she cries, her free hand over her heart. "You gave me a fright, sister! Were you having a nightmare?"

Embarrassed and at my wit's end, I begin to cry. "I'm in a nightmare all the time, Emily," I manage, trying to make her understand even though she never will. "I just want to wake up."

I am not even a mother, yet at the same time I am the worst one who has ever lived.

"You're suffering through one of the most horrid types of loss there is," she whispers, and pulls me close so she can stroke my hair while I weep. "It's only natural for you to feel this way right now."

I want to ask her if it's natural for my child's soul to be so unsettled that it lingers around to haunt me. I want to ask her if it's natural for me not to be fully certain

which parts of my life are real and which are not. I want
to ask her if she'll take Pa's rifle and end things for me.

"I'm fine," I whisper, and Emily squeezes my hand
again. "Or I will be, anyway."

My sister offers to stay with me inside for the remainder of the day, but suddenly all I want to do is get out
of these dampened sheets and go outside, where I can
breathe in the endlessness of the open sky. I get dressed
quickly, and we go out together, and Emily looks surprised when I suggest we play a game with Joanna and
Charles.

It feels good to have an excuse to avoid Hannah for
a little longer, even if I am still pinching with cramps
and tired enough to sleep for a week. I make sure not to
look back at the stretch of prairie that rests behind the
cabin, where I saw the baby in the dark. I don't want to
see anything else. I must regain control.

Later that afternoon, Emily and I are sitting on the
fence with the children when I see her face change as
she looks toward the forest.

Zeke is in the distance, riding on horseback, about
halfway between the cabin and the trees. He is alone.
There are big covered buckets resting on each side of the
saddle, presumably to collect water in. Emily watches
him grow closer from the shade of her sunbonnet with
an unsure expression. Pa doesn't look too thrilled at
the sight of the boy, but Ma and the children wave and
call out *hello*.

"Hello, neighbors!" Zeke calls as he approaches, and the children continue to wave wildly from where they stand on the fence. "You've certainly cleaned up that yard, haven't you?"

"Look inside when you go to get your water," Pa says from where he whittles a design into the leg of a chair. "You won't recognize it, guaranteed."

"Let's hope not," Zeke says jokingly.

Emily shifts her weight uncomfortably beside me while she looks over at Zeke. He rides into the front clearing, dismounts his horse and tips his hat to Emily. She smiles, but not as brightly as she did the other times he was here. Warm satisfaction washes over my heart. *Too bad, Zeke.* I fight the urge to ask him about the knock on the window the other night.

"How are things, Emily Verner?" Zeke asks, low enough for Ma and Pa not to hear.

"Very well, thank you," she replies quaintly. "And how is the doctor?"

"The same," Zeke says, then looks over his shoulder to the forest line. Why does he always look like he's anticipating something? "He's in Elmwood, at the moment—"

"Were you here the other night?" I ask, cutting him off and ignoring my better judgment. Zeke and Emily look at me in surprise. "On the prairie, I mean. Did you knock on our window and then run away?"

Zeke's eyebrows furrow at my accusation. "It wasn't me," he says after an uncomfortable pause. He removes the buckets from the sides of the saddle quickly, purposefully avoiding my gaze, then starts walking back toward the well pump. "I haven't been here since I came with my father."

He doesn't ask more about the incident, doesn't wonder aloud who would knock on our window at night and then run away, and doesn't even attempt to woo Emily with some other flirtatious line or gesture, which only makes me feel quite certain that he is the one who did it.

It had to have been him, I knew I didn't imagine it, *I didn't*, and it most certainly wasn't the baby with the animal eyes.

"Why do you still think he did that?" Emily asks after Zeke's out of earshot, not angry, just genuinely curious. "I remember that night very well. I didn't hear—"

"So, just because *you* didn't hear anything, nothing happened?" I say, more shrilly than I intend. My sister frowns. "I know what I heard, Emily. Zeke and his father are the only ones who live around here for miles and miles."

She looks aggravated now, but holds her tongue.

"What?" I challenge, trying to get her to stop being so God-cursedly perfect all the time. "You don't want to disagree with me? Afraid that you'll push me over the edge because my baby died?"

Emily's mouth drops open, and I instantly regret that I said it.

"I'm sorry," I say, and put my hand on hers. I only just

got her back, I mustn't ruin it now just because of Zeke. "I'm so sorry, sister. That wasn't fair."

"No, it wasn't," she replies, looking after Zeke as he passes by the front door without looking in. "But it's all right. I understand. Amanda, are you *sure* you're feeling all right?"

"I'm exhausted and sore. What more do you want me to say about it?"

"I'm..." Emily's voice lowers even more. "I'm not talking about the baby."

"Emily," I say, and close my eyes in frustration. "I would tell you if I wasn't."

I lie because I only just got her back, and I refuse to risk distancing myself by reawakening the fear that clouded her eyes when I told her about the devil in the woods.

The children run to follow Zeke, asking questions about the forest and begging to know when he'll come back for the scary stories he promised Emily last time he was here.

The scary stories, I'd almost forgotten. After Zeke disappears around the corner of the cabin, I look, finally, to the spot where I saw the haunt of the infant. The grasses bend back and forth at the mercy of the breezes, and my stomach turns at the knowledge of what is on the ground there, *in* it. I wonder what types of stories Zeke knows.

I wonder if any of them sound like mine.

"You really should come for those stories, you know," I say once he's back at his horse, trying my best to sound earnest. "I would love to hear some about the prairie."

Emily sighs from beside me, then crosses her arms over her chest. She thinks that I'm fooling.

Zeke fumbles with the saddle straps that wrap around the closed water containers. He pauses before turning slowly to look at me. "How do you know that there are any?"

"Well, you know," I say, and shrug. "I can only imagine how the isolation of this place could cause people to go mad."

Zeke stares at me, his expression serious. "Where did you hear that?"

"She didn't hear it anywhere," Emily cuts in apologetically. She doesn't believe that I actually want to hear any stories; judging by the angry nudge of her boot, she thinks that I'm teasing Zeke, maybe even trying to get him to admit to knocking on the window. "She's especially tired today and wasn't feeling well earlier—"

"I'm fine, sister," I insist. "Really." I look back to Zeke. "I just thought it'd be nice to get away and enjoy a story or two. I guess I could use the distraction." It's only a half lie.

Emily looks a bit more convinced. "Well, if you're sure you really want to..."

I shrug. "It's better than sitting on a fence with nothing to look at but our own shadows."

Zeke and Emily laugh, and I know that I have won.

"Please, Zeke?" Charles says from where he stands, petting the horse's nose. "I love spooky stories!"

"Yes, please!" adds Joanna. "We can even take the *really* scary ones."

Zeke removes his hat to wipe the sweat from his forehead, deliberating, then puts it back on. "We'll do it tomorrow afternoon," he says. "But only if Emily agrees to sit by me so I don't get too scared."

My sister blushes, of course. "Maybe I will," Emily says. "And maybe I won't. I guess we'll have to see if you actually show up."

This makes Zeke laugh. I hate the sound of it just as much as I do the redness in Emily's cheeks. I swear, something good had better come of this. Something useful.

"That's fair enough," he says. "I should be going, now."

"Why in the afternoon?" Joanna asks as he mounts his horse. "Aren't you supposed to tell spooky stories at night, around a fire?"

Zeke's smile flickers away for just a second. He has to know *something*. Why else would he avoid Jo's question? I knew it. He waves to Pa and thanks him for the water. "See you tomorrow afternoon, everyone. So long, Emily Verner."

"So long, Zeke." Emily grins, and then he's going. When she sees me eyeing her, the grin fades.

"What?"

"Nothing." I take a deep breath to release the pressure in my chest.

"Oh, please," she says. "Just because you're hurting doesn't mean I won't call you out in a lie."

"That's fair enough," I say, mocking Zeke in a flawless impression. "Fair enough, Emily Verner. Now, if you wouldn't mind coming on over here to sit next to me, just so I can smell your heavenly hair..."

My sister erupts into laughter. "Oh, my Lord," she manages in between breathes. "You are absolutely ridiculous."

"You can't be cross anymore," I say with a smile. "I made you laugh."

"Oh, wretched."

Pa abandons his project for a moment to take a swig of whiskey from the flask on his belt. He watches Zeke get smaller into the distance. "Why didn't he look inside the cabin?" he calls over to us. "He said he was going to, and then he never did. You would have thought he'd be interested in seeing it."

"I'm sure he'll look next time he comes," Emily says. "He seemed to be in a bit of a hurry."

"It's so strange that they insist on using that pump." Pa takes another sloppy gulp that leaves his beard sparkling with amber droplets of liquor. "I don't think they need the water. They told me in Elmwood that those woods are veined with creeks."

"It's much cleaner than creek water." Emily looks insulted on Zeke's behalf. "They probably only use it for drinking and use the creek water for everything else."

"Maybe," Pa says. "Anyway, did I hear something about scary stories? You'd better go inside and ask your ma about it. You know how she feels about those sorts of things." He secures the flask back onto his belt and returns to his work. "If you do end up going, take the snake catcher."

The snake catcher is a contraption Pa rigged up that consists of a wire loop at the end of a walking stick. You pull the end of the wire to close the loop, trapping any snakes that might be trying to strike. So far, nobody has used it to catch a real snake.

"Ma just said that she doesn't want the stories to be satanic," I assure him. "And we will take the snake catcher."

Pa goes back to work, and my sister and I hop down from the fence.

"I know what you did," Emily says as we make our way to go talk to Ma inside the cabin. "And I have to say, thank you, sister. I know you don't like Zeke, but you still put my feelings ahead of yours, and actively at that. You are truly the dearest friend I could ever hope for."

Her words have the opposite effect on me than what I think she intended. Leave it to Emily to give me the benefit of the doubt in the times when I deserve it the least. I wonder for a moment what would have become of my sister if I had run away with Henry. Would she finally be able to see people for who they really are? Would it have benefited her to be here without me? The dreamy smile on her face suggests so, and it makes me feel like I deserve everything that's been happening.

"You're welcome," I say, sealing my fate in Hell. "I love you, Emily."

SIXTEEN

The place where we meet up with Zeke the following afternoon is halfway between the cabin and the forest. He is working to get a fire started in the rock-lined pit when we all arrive. Halved logs that are crumbling with dead bark are arranged in a widened triangle around the area.

I didn't hear the infant crying last night, but I won't allow myself to feed any hope that might suggest nothing is wrong here. The emptiness inside of me, both physically and not, is still new and strange enough that I can never feel truly certain about anything that is happening, or what came before this. What exactly do I hope to learn from whatever story Zeke is about to tell?

"I've always known this spot was here, but have never used it until now," Zeke admits, his hands on his knees as he bends down to poke the fire and make sure it kindles. I sit on one of the logs, and the children scramble up on top of another. "I think it's probably the old camping place of somebody who traveled through the prairie at one point. Either way, a little bird somewhere told me that you just *cannot* tell a scary story without the presence of a fire, so here we are."

Joanna tugs on the tie of her sunbonnet and grins shyly. "I guess it's a good thing we came in the daytime," she says. "Ma said we wouldn't have been allowed to come if it had been at night."

"Your ma is a smart woman," Zeke says. He sits down on the last log and smiles hopefully up at Emily. She looks back with an arched brow and a half grin before sitting beside me. I want to laugh, but I mustn't anger Zeke. I need to hear what else has happened on this prairie. "There are lots of animals and other things that like to hunt at night."

What other things? I want to ask, but I hold my tongue. *Tell me what is happening to me.*

"So today," Zeke continues, "I thought I'd share a story with you that my grandfather used to tell me when I was younger, whenever I was acting especially rowdy or cross. He lived in the same cabin that we do now, you see. He lived near the prairie his entire life."

Zeke tells us about Jasper Kensington, who was well-known and equally liked around Elmwood, a family man who made a living by hauling in wood from the forest near his cabin and carving it into beautiful pieces of furniture to be sold by one of the town vendors.

"That's what our pa does!" Joanna gasps, and Zeke

suppresses a smile. For a moment I become worried; I hope he isn't making something up as he goes along, twisting important things around just so that the story is more personalized and likely to scare the children. I need him to tell the story like he heard it, I need to know if my mind is breaking. I saw it on his face yesterday when I mentioned the prairie. He has information that could help me.

"He came into town every other Friday," Zeke begins, the heat from the fire smearing his features together. "And never missed a day in nearly fifteen years."

Here we go.

"Until one especially cruel summer. The vendors expecting Mr. Kensington that day simply assumed he came down with something or needed to tend to a matter at home. Things happen out here on the prairie," Zeke tells us, his voice ominous. "Things happen out here all the time." The children's eyes are aglow with anticipation.

I lean forward, praying that I'll be able to somehow find help in Zeke's words.

"So, while surprising, Jasper's absence caused no serious alarm. Until four days later, that is, when he stumbled into the center of town without a horse, limping and sunburned and rambling bouts of complete and utter nonsense.

"He was smiling," Zeke continues. "Smiling like a madman and laughing to the sky as if he'd drunk more than a few fingers of whiskey. He was covered from head to toe in blood, and he was carrying a scythe."

"Oooh!" Joanna cries, delightfully repulsed.

"What's a scythe?" asks Charles.

"They use it to harvest wheat," Joanna spurts excitedly, hardly able to contain herself. "They are *so* scary, Charles, they look like giant claws! I saw one on the mountain once when Pa took me into—"

"Let Zeke go on," I urge the children. "I want to know what happens next."

Emily waits quietly from where she sits beside me. Zeke nods.

"'I killed my girls!' he cried gleefully to a group of children who were playing jacks by the well. 'Their little skulls broke like hen's eggs, why yes, they did, and spilled their contents generously! I *tasted* them!'"

"Ewwww," Joanna and Charles cry out together, and hook their arms around each other.

"Well, isn't that lovely," Emily says, disgust evident in her expression.

"The children screamed and scattered," Zeke continues, "catching the attention of townspeople and stable workers and vendors and my grandfather, who had been sitting outside while practicing his Biblical catechisms. The commotion caught the attention of Sheriff Stoekel real quick, a man who'd been quite fond of Kensington and spent many afternoons laughing over cards and cigars with him.

"The sheriff held his hand over the gun on his belt, but didn't draw as he moved slowly to the cackling man covered in red.

"'Now, what's this about, Jasper?' Mr. Stoekel yelled. 'What's all this about you killing your girls?'

"Kensington faced the sheriff in a jerky motion," Zeke says. "But he just started laughing all the harder. 'My sweet little girls,' he managed to gasp. 'And my good wife, too. The claws told me to break their little teeth out with rocks, to see their insides and paint the walls with them, and they struggled, Sheriff, *oh, how they struggled!*'"

"Oh, my," Joanna says softly. Charles bites his lip.

"That was when Stoekel drew his gun," Zeke continues. "He said, 'Drop the scythe, Jasper, and let us take you to a holding cell and get some water in you. What you're saying is nonsense. You're mad from dehydration.'

"The Kensington man fell to his knees, the laughter gone. Suddenly he seemed petrified. The scythe, slicked with crimson and sun-hardened chunks of yellow and white, fell from his hand and into the dirt. He started begging the sheriff for forgiveness. He was convinced that there were demons in the prairie, that he didn't kill his family at all. But they *were* dead, all of them, just like Jasper said. The sheriff found the bodies inside the family's cabin. It was a bloodbath."

The children wait for him to continue, their arms still

wound tightly around each other. Zeke sits up straight and sighs. The story is over.

"That," Emily says, "was quite the spine-tingler."

"It was gross." Joanna crinkles her nose.

"But what happened to him?" I ask from the halved log, my hands clasped together in a frightened fist in my lap. "What happened to Jasper Kensington?"

Zeke looks into the fire, unblinking. "I'm not exactly sure. My grandfather, er—" his hand goes to rub his neck "—he never told the story past that point."

"I bet he became a ghost!" Charles says. He wiggles his finger in Joanna's ear, and she screeches. "I bet he wanders all around the prairie at night, dragging chains and saying *ooooh! oooooh!*"

Zeke chuckles. "Perhaps you are right. I could have sworn yesterday on my way home that I saw chain marks in the dirt."

Charles's face goes from entertained to terrified in a second.

"Joking, of course," Zeke says. "You won't find any ghosts on this prairie."

I am not relieved, or satisfied, for what am I to gather from this—that I will continue to lose my mind and eventually kill my own family? The cries in the night have startled me so, as did the sight of the infant standing upright in the dark, but I haven't been *hurt* by anything, nobody has. I haven't wanted to hurt anyone.

But you have.

I remember the moment after the miscarriage, how I stepped outside when Hannah was crying, how I broke open the skin of my palms and felt as though I would have done anything to silence her. But that wasn't anything real, right? It was the sorrow of losing my own child that drove me to the thought, I wouldn't have truly done anything to hurt her. I couldn't have.

You've been praying for her death since before *the prairie.* How despicable that I repeat this to myself as a comfort.

It's no wonder the devil came for my soul in the woods.

"There *is* one other thing my grandfather always said," Zeke mentions, staring at Emily to ensure that she's listening. "He said that even though the prairie wasn't safe, the forest always would be."

"How convenient," my sister laughs. "It's safe where you live, but the poor Verners are doomed!"

He doesn't look amused by her joke. A wild thought crosses my mind. *He thinks I'm going to hurt them. He's trying to protect Emily from me.* Zeke stands and kicks the fire out with the loose dirt that surrounds the rocky perimeter. "I should be going now," he says. "But I have to say, it was pretty fun to see the faces of the children. You two know it was just a story, don't you?"

Joanna and Charles nod, but don't look entirely convinced.

"It is, right?" I ask, standing, too, my voice quickening. "Zeke? It's only a story."

"Amanda," Emily says, confused. "What's wrong?"

"Of course," Zeke answers as he walks to his horse without meeting my gaze. "Of course it is."

"You're leaving so suddenly." Emily stands up and brushes the bark from the back of her skirt. "But still, I enjoyed myself, Zeke. Maybe we can do it another time?"

She is trying not to sound desperate for my sake, but still I can sense that she is pining for him. And by the way he turns around, looks into her eyes and steps close enough to kiss her if he wanted, it's clear he feels the same way. This is when I fully realize that the post boy from the mountain never loved me at all.

The intensity between my sister and the boy who lives in the forest is unmistakable, even after such a short time. It's something I never had with Henry, and the envy is almost physically painful.

"Why don't we gather in the forest next time?" He looks to the children now, too, and me. "We could tell stories in the shade of the trees and not have to worry about the snakes. Please?"

I think of Zeke's shaking hands, holding the shotgun when I first saw him outside the cabin. I think of his hesitant glances and unanswered questions and the urgency in his voice now. He is afraid of the prairie. Does he know that I'm losing my mind?

"Maybe we can sometime." Emily shrugs, looking to me for input. "If Amanda wants to, of course."

"Yes," I say, suddenly feeling very vulnerable out here in the grass. I want to get back to the cabin, right now. "Sure."

Zeke nods, takes Emily's hand in his for just a second, then turns back for his horse. He mounts in a smooth, swift motion that reminds me a little bit of Henry.

"So long, Verner family," he calls over his shoulder. "Watch out for ghosts tonight."

SEVENTEEN

By the time a few days have passed, I've learned that constantly anticipating something terrible happening is almost as bad, if not worse, than the occurrence of an actual incident. Something is building up in the air, something quiet but distinct, a vast heaviness that I cannot quite put my finger on.

Pa has just returned from a trade and supply run to Elmwood, and announces that the rest of the day will be dedicated to rest and relaxation, with an especially fancy dinner to celebrate how well received his pieces were.

"Nobody works today." He grins, handing out horehound candy and dried blackberries that remind me of the mountains. Ma drags her rocking chair out into the front clearing so she can sit and look into the endless sea of flatlands, which are currently being shaded by thick smears of dark clouds that cover the sun. Since we've arrived, the heat has receded if only just a little bit, and the winds bring a welcomed rush of additional comfort.

I haven't been able to get the story of Jasper Kensington out of my mind, and now I second-guess every thought that I have. I vow to myself, over and over again, that no matter how unraveled my mind becomes, I will not hurt my family.

My thoughts cannot trigger evil, I think. *My thoughts cannot invite demons.*

I also haven't been able to stop thinking about Hannah. Since my period of brief closeness with my baby sister, I feel as though she is always seeking me out, and even though looking at her still reminds me of what I've lost, I am also being steadily poisoned with the worry of losing my mind and hurting someone.

Because even if what Zeke said about the prairie isn't true, clearly *something* terrible and irreversible has happened to cause such hysteria within me. How long will I be haunted like this?

If it becomes real to me, the others could suffer for it, and that is what petrifies me. I cannot let it happen.

If I tried to explain a word of this to Ma or Pa, they would think that I was a witch or something of the sort, no way around it. And I thought their reaction to my pregnancy would be catastrophic. It's hard to believe that I was so absorbed with that problem, so distressed and hopeless and sure of my fate.

I would kill to have that problem again.

In the early hours of the afternoon, it begins to rain, and everybody takes shelter in the cabin. I go to the area of the floor where Hannah sits exploring the giant head of the grizzly rug. She seems to like the teeth the most, and runs her fingers up and down the hardened gums and jaw of the beast. I slide my hand over her chubby calf, and she turns on her knees to wrap her tiny arms around my neck with an excited shriek.

"*Mlaaaarugh*," she cries out. I pull her close to me, kiss her fuzzy eyebrow.

"Hello again, sweetness," I whisper against her hair. I hum a low tone for as long as my breath will go, and the baby lays her head happily on my chest to feel it. I transition into a hymn called "Come, Holy Ghost," slowly and gently, rocking the baby back and forth and willing her to feel and understand my thoughts as she falls asleep.

I do not want you to die. I am so sorry that I ever did. I take it back. I love you. I love you. I love you.

This needs to be over now, I think to myself in desperation. *The madness must stop at once.*

"Oh, my," Ma says from the rocking chair, her voice fragile. I look up at her to see that her eyes have gone misty, and her knitting rests forgotten on her lap. "That is just precious, Amanda. What a sight of true and wondrous joy."

I don't realize until now that there are tears on my

cheeks. Emily has looked up from her button collection, but doesn't appear nearly as touched as Ma. In fact, she seems worried.

"There's no reason to cry, Amanda," Pa says from where he sits on a stool, whittling a new handle for his hunting knife. "That baby knows how much you love her."

As if you would know, I think. *You understand her about as well as you understand me.*

"I'm fine," I say. "I'm just sorry I didn't help you more with the baby until recently, Ma."

"Oh, dearest." Ma nods sharply and begins working on her knitting again. "There is nothing to apologize for."

Hannah's eyes are closed into tiny half-moons. I continue to rock her, even after the song is finished. Her hand grazes my arm up and down with such tenderness. I imagine how horrible it would feel to hurt her.

It will never happen.

Suddenly, the baby's hand stops stroking the fabric of my dress and goes limp. Her blank expression twists into one of concern, and she moves her head to a different part of my chest, as if she's listening to something. Of course she isn't listening to anything, she doesn't hear, I am imagining it.

Hannah whimpers, then wriggles out of my grip so that she's sitting beside me. Her eyebrows are pulled together, and her gray eyes widen without blinking as she leans over and sets her ear directly over my womb. I look up in surprise to see if Emily is witnessing it, if anybody is, but they've all gone back to what they were doing, and I am alone in my wonder.

I watch Hannah's face as she sits still, her expression becoming steadily more afraid.

"Hannah?" I whisper, no longer entirely sure that she can't hear me. My heart skips in my chest when she looks up sharply in response.

Her eyes have no whites. They are entirely clouded with gray, like the eyes of a dead fish, like the baby standing outside in the grass that night.

The baby begins to scream. She reels backward from me and begins crawling away as fast as she can, stumbling over the fabric of her skirt at first. Her eyes are back to how they always are, but I'm still so startled that it takes me a moment to lean forward and try and help her. As soon as my hands are on her, the screams intensify.

"Just start humming again," Ma says nonchalantly from the chair. "Just grab her and—"

But I've already pulled my hands away in reaction to the screams, and Hannah bounds forward off the grizzly-bear rug and into the mouth of the fireplace. I expect her to stop as soon as she feels the heat from the flames, but to my horror, she keeps going.

She's going to crawl into the fire.

"Grab her!" Ma cries from the rocking chair and hurls herself forward. She gets to the baby right in time, sweeps her up so quickly that a flurry of ashes swirl into the air after her feet. "Oh, my God, she almost went in, oh, my God..."

"Is she all right?" I stand up quickly and go after Ma, who snaps to face me with a look of anger and revulsion.

"How could you just let her crawl in like that? I *saw* you, she got away from you and you just *let her—*"

"Ma!" Emily says in surprise. "Amanda wouldn't do that on purpose!"

"Of course I didn't do it on purpose," I plead, trying to stroke Hannah's hair, but every time I come close she gets even deeper into the fit. "It all happened so fast—"

"Your sister almost died," Ma yells into my face. I've never seen her lose control like this, none of us have. The children sit in their toy corner, still as statues as they look on with big worried eyes. "After everything she's been through, she could have died due to your carelessness!"

I step away, trying hard not to cry, and as soon as I back away the baby falls silent. She doesn't want me near her anymore. Why? What have I done? What did she hear in my womb?

"That is enough, Susan." Pa says it with such force and

intensity that Ma pulls herself together in an instant. "Hannah is fine. Look at her. It was a close call, that's all. And now you've frightened poor Amanda into thinking she's responsible for something that didn't even happen. This was to be a day of rest and relaxation, and it will be. This conflict is over now."

Ma looks ashamed. "Daughter, I apologize, I was just so scared, my baby..."

"It's all right, Ma," I say. The baby's eyes are closed. "You don't need to explain. I...I don't know why Hannah dislikes being close to me all of a sudden."

I tell everybody that I need some fresh air and stand just outside the door, in the drizzling rain. I let it fall into my hair and dress, barely feeling it, not knowing what to do next. If Hannah had crawled into the fire, would it have been my fault? My doing? Did something inside of me *want* to let her crawl in?

No. Something happened in there. Hannah sensed something. Her eyes changed. She became terrified of me.

The door to the cabin cracks open, and Emily steps out to join me.

"What is the matter with you?" she says. "Something has been bothering you for days now."

How do I even begin? I'm terrified of myself. I almost feel nervous for my sister, for being out here with me alone like this. Who knows what sorts of things will continue to happen around me?

"At first I thought it was because of your baby," Emily continues. "But ever since we went to visit with Zeke at the fire pit I've realized that it has to be something else. You're not acting sad, sister, you're acting *scared*. What is it? I thought there were to be no more secrets between us?" From the distance comes a roll of thunder.

I cannot take it anymore. The secrets, the lies, the guilt, the fear. I have to find a way to let them all go. I can no longer manage to believe that keeping it all inside will somehow protect them. I am no longer able to figure this out on my own. I need to get it out to Emily, and I need to get it out now. If I am to lose my mind, someone will need to understand what is happening. Someone will need to protect my family from me.

"I'm going mad," I say, and already I feel some release. "I hear an infant crying at night, outside the cabin, and I saw something standing in the grass where I miscarried—"

"The nightmares will cease eventually," Emily promises, and takes my hand in hers. "Don't be too afraid of them. You are strong, Amanda."

"You don't understand," I say, and start sniffling. The rain lessens, and I hear the sound of Ma rustling around some cooking pots inside. "They weren't nightmares. I really heard the cries. I went outside in the night, and

I saw a baby in the prairie, I saw it with my own eyes, Emily, and I was awake. I *was*. And the knock on the window—"

"Listen to me carefully, sister." Emily cuts me off, her voice slowing. "This is just like that time on the mountain. There was no knock on the window that night. You imagined it."

"Then I imagined it!" I give up, throwing my hands in the air, making my sister jump. "But if I am, then would you mind telling me why? Just now, with Hannah, her eyes changed, they looked like they belonged to a dead fish. I think she's in danger, Emily, I think that Hannah is in danger—"

"Stop this," she insists. "This is all coming from your stress, and your fear. You can't even rest properly because of it! I feel you on the other side of the mattress, tossing and turning all through the night! You're not even sleeping at all, are you? That's why you're hearing things again—"

"Emily," I whisper. "This isn't the same thing as what happened on the mountain, or at least, I don't think so—"

"But how would you know?" my sister challenges. "You've endured an extraordinary amount of stress, your mind could still be vulnerable from last winter. And you haven't gotten a decent amount of sleep since... since...you know."

"Since my baby was taken from me?"

"Yes."

I don't continue for a moment. I was wrong before, when I thought that nobody had been hurt in the midst of all of this, when I was trying to convince myself that I could endure the madness forever. I was hurt. My baby was hurt.

You prayed for it.

"You have guilt over the baby, don't you?" Emily says, peering into my face. "You think it was your fault that it happened."

"I didn't want the baby, Emily. I was so mad when I found out I was with child. I wanted it to end."

"It wasn't your fault."

"Maybe."

"Listen to me," Emily urges. "Please. You'd been through a hard time. You needed a distraction to survive. The outcome was unfortunate, but it happened all the same."

I don't reply, and she takes my hand. "Just promise me that tonight you'll take some deep breaths, you'll stop thinking about the boy from the mountain and whatever sounds you've been hearing in the night, that you'll force yourself to rest. *Truly* rest. Just like after you saw that thing in the woods."

"And if I continue hearing things? Seeing things?"

Emily pauses, studying me.

"I am so very worried about you," my sister says gently, squeezing my hand. "The circles under your eyes are dark enough to look like bruises, Amanda. You've grown so thin. The color is washed out of you. You have got to promise me that if this continues, if even one more thing happens that seems out of the ordinary, you'll tell Ma and Pa so they can take you to Doctor Jacobson. And tonight you must *sleep*."

I feel as tired as I must look. I just want her to be right, more than anything in the world, I want to let go and forget about all of this. I only need some sleep, perhaps even a doctor. Either way, everything will turn out fine in the end.

"All right," I agree, and Emily hugs me tight. "Just for tonight, I'll listen to you."

"Thank you," she breathes, relieved. "I've never given you rotten advice before, have I?"

"No."

"Precisely." The embrace ends, and she points back to the cabin. "Let's go help Ma get started with supper. The baby is sleeping by now, so there's nothing to worry about. Just *relax*, sister, relax your mind and body. Everything will be all right. Hannah is not in danger."

I nod, even though something still doesn't seem right, and turn to head back inside. I am tired of trying to figure this out, for now.

EIGHTEEN

An hour later, Ma and I are searing thick slices of salt pork that Pa purchased in town. The crisping meat spits enthusiastically when I turn it with my fork, and it smells lovely. Ma has apologized for getting cross with me at least four times since I came in from outside, and after finding me a dry dress to wear, hugged me tight and told me she loved me. I pay close attention to my breathing, keeping it long and slow and deep.

Joanna and Emily use wooden forks to smash the potatoes we boiled previously into a smooth, creamy mush against the sides of a big bowl. The steam rises from the mash as they stir in a boiled garlic clove and spoonful of seasonings. Charles sets out a plate of cold cornmeal cakes left over from lunch and smears them with honey.

Once the meat is out of the pan, we use a little of the starchy potato water to loosen the browned meat bits in the pan for gravy.

Not even I can resist the unbeatable power of a hot, filling meal. We all listen to Ma and Pa exchange light-hearted chatter while we eat, about things like hunting some deer meat from the woods soon for stew and dumplings or attempting an apple pie in the new fireplace, since it's so roomy and everything. Charles sucks the hot pork grease from his fingers, and Ma doesn't even scold him for it.

Afterward we lie around with full bellies, drunk from all the food, and Pa pulls out his old fiddle to play and sing us a tune about fishing for trout with a big, fat worm. We clap along to the fast-paced jig, Ma's hands laced over Hannah's to guide her so she can join along, and the baby falls into a fit of giggles. Desperate not to spoil the mood, I take special care to keep far away from her so she doesn't fall into another fit.

By Pa's fourth song, a slow and beautiful piece about twinkling stars in a black blanket of sky, the baby is lying against Ma's shoulder and sleeping, her thick lashes against her cheeks. I wonder if she'll ever love me again.

Bedtime comes not long after that, and Ma gently takes the sleeping baby and lays her on the far side of the mattress they share with Pa. Joanna, Charles, Emily and I line up on our own mattress, and all face the same way so we can tickle the back of each other's necks and shoulders until we're too tired to lift our arms. I keep

breathing, keep repeating Emily's words to myself—
everything will be all right.

The room quiets, the heavy breathing gets replaced
by snores, and I find myself drifting out to the faint red
glow of the dying fireplace and the lingering smell of
crispy seasoned pork and freshly built floor. Maybe it
won't be too hard to ignore all that's happened if it goes
away now, fades away like a bad dream, just like Henry
and my baby. My last thought before I fall asleep is, *If my
baby was a girl, I would have named her Emily.*

Hannah is screaming.

It feels like only a second has passed, but the fire is
completely dead now, and the baby's cries tear through
the pitch-black that surrounds us. They aren't like her
normal cries, either, but louder and harder than I've
ever heard any child scream in my entire life, like she's
in unbearable pain.

"What is—" Ma's voice is cut off when the screams intensify. The children and Emily and I all sit up in sleepy
panic.

"Edmund!" My ma is suddenly screaming, right along
with the baby. "Light a candle! Oh, my Lord—Hannah—
There's something all over Hannah!"

"What's happening?" Joanna cries from my side and
blindly grabs at me in the dark. I pull her shaking body
close to my own.

Pa darts across the dark cabin, trips over the rocking

chair, and in ten seconds more he is scrambling to light the oil lamp from the corner of the room. Suddenly the light flickers on, and the room is filled with the softest yellow glow, hardly enough to see clearly, but I tell Joanna to hug Charles while I scramble up and make my way over to the still-screaming Hannah.

She sounds to be in complete agony, and from where I stand I can see that she is flailing against the mattress, hard. The closer I get, the more confused I become; the baby appears to be covered in a shimmering black liquid.

I follow the trail of it that spills over the side of the mattress, squinting, and reach out to touch it. I poke my finger into the black just as Pa reaches the bed, and the light from the kerosene lamp shows me the truth just in time. It's not liquid that's covering Hannah and the bed around her, and Ma realizes this at the same instant I do. We both scream.

Ants.

Red prairie ants, the size of bullets, coming up from a tiny hole next to the mattress and covering my flailing baby sister from head to toe while she gasps for air. The crimson ants skitter over the white mattress in a panicked reaction to the light. Hannah's violent movements slow, and she begins to twitch.

I hear myself let out a sob and desperately try to brush the disgusting things away from her chubby face while

Ma does the same. They cling to her skin, eating her alive, trying to burrow themselves into her eyes and ears and mouth.

Pa nearly drops the lantern in shock. He bellows for us to move away from the mattress. My hands are on fire and dotted with the disgusting creatures, and I slap at myself wildly to prevent them from moving up my arms.

Ma cries out in pain, her hands covered as well, but she lifts Hannah in the dark and stumbles over to the dish tub filled with water, still cloudy with food chunks and grease from tonight's dinner, and dunks the silent baby completely under.

Emily leads Joanna and Charles to the corner farthest away from the mattresses while Ma tears off Hannah's soaked clothing. There are more ants underneath her sleeping gown, clinging to her like sewing pins, and without hesitation Ma dunks the baby into the filthy water again.

I have a clean, dry rag waiting for Ma, and she snatches it from me gratefully. She rubs the baby down with it, and Pa leans closer with the lamp to inspect the damage. The baby moans and very slowly lifts her hand up, searching for someone to help her, and I take it and hold it against my neck that is covered in tears.

"*Huuuuuuuuuh*," I try to hum in a smooth, calming rhythm, but I'm breathing so hard that the sigh breaks apart into a couple of panicked huffs. I want to see God's face, just so I can spit in it.

"She needs help," Ma says in a shaking voice. "She's going to die, Edmund. She needs help *now*."

Sure enough, Hannah's face and limbs are so swollen that they are almost unrecognizable. The puffy skin is as scarlet as the monsters that did this to her, and completely covered in raised white bumps. Her fat little hand goes limp and falls away from my face. She isn't breathing, really; just letting out little puffs of air in a series of quick, sharp wheezes.

"Doctor Jacobson," I manage through my tears. "Take Hannah to the woods, maybe he can help her!"

Pa goes into action immediately, and has Rocky saddled and ready to go in less than five minutes. He promises that even if Hannah needs to stay at the doctor's cabin, he will come back to let us know what is happening before dawn. He takes the baby from Ma, kisses her, then pulls himself up and onto the horse with his free hand.

"Stay away from the ants until I get back," he commands. "Wait outside or in the wagon if they start to spread out."

He is gone. The winds in the prairie are dead for once, and the only sound to accompany the shock in the air is Charles's gentle weeping.

"Is Hannah going to die?" Joanna sniffs and pulls at

her dark, curly hair with both hands. "God wouldn't do that, right, Ma? Hannah can't die."

"I do not know, child." Ma stares after Pa, her eyes lost and unblinking. "If only I did."

I turn from the sight of Pa on Rocky, loping toward the forest line by the light of the moon. Emily looks on, wide-eyed, pale, like the time I was seven and she was five and a grizzly bear wandered, snarling, into the front clearing of our cabin. I don't know what to do, or say, or think.

This cursed prairie.

"I need to take care of the ants," I hear myself say. Ma doesn't move, or speak, or turn away from the forest. "I'm going to smash every last one of them."

"Wait." Emily snaps into reality and grabs my elbow. "Maybe you shouldn't. Your hands..."

My hands. I haven't even looked at them, or felt them really, since I first realized I was being bitten. They are swollen, puffy, covered in bites, but it's nothing compared to what Hannah is going through, and I cannot find it in myself to admit how much they hurt.

"My hands are fine," I say.

I go into the cabin, slip on my work boots and take the abandoned kerosene lamp that is sitting by the door. Emily commands Joanna and Charles to wait at the door while she follows me slowly to the mattress that Ma and Pa and Hannah share. When we get near, I ready my foot to stomp down on the mass of squirming insects as soon as I see them. I lift the lantern and hold my breath.

All of the ants are gone, every last one of them. It's as if they were never even here at all.

NINETEEN

When Ma was six months into her pregnancy with Hannah, the snow started.

It fell in fat, fluffy flakes, the sticky kind that quickly piled up enough to make snowmen and angels and ice treats drizzled with maple syrup. At first, it was fun. Emily and I played in the powder with Joanna and Charles while Ma, swollen in the belly but rosy in the cheeks, brewed a pot of hot tea with honey for when we returned.

"Don't stay out too late with them, Amanda!" Ma yelled from the open cabin door as Emily and I walked up the slope of the mountain with Pa's old sled. "I don't want you to catch your deaths out there."

"Just one more, Ma!" Emily yelled back through the slow-falling wall of thickened snowflakes. She set the sled down and began adjusting her mittens with her teeth. "All right, Jo. Get on."

Joanna cautiously lifted one leg over the sled and fell

onto the seat, near the back to leave the front open for Charles. I picked him up and set him on top, and Joanna wrapped her arms around his middle and pulled.

"Hold on tight, Joanna," Charles instructed very seriously, his hands clenched around the front rope so hard that I knew his knuckles must be white beneath his mittens. Ever since he found out that he would no longer be the baby of the family, he was determined to show us all that he was indeed a big boy now. My heart warmed at the sight of such pure courage.

I planted my boot in front of the top corner of the sled, then stood to straighten my back and check out the clearing below to our left. I thought that Emily was holding on to the opposite corner with her own foot, but I realized as soon as Joanna shifted her weight that I was very wrong. The sled was sucked away from us in an instant.

The trees.

We hadn't readjusted the sled to face the open space down the side of the mountain, the only safe place around the cabin to ride. I prayed to God that Joanna would lose her balance and fall off the back of the sled, taking Charles with her in an effort to save herself.

She didn't. Joanna teetered for a second, giving me hope, but her back stayed strong in the end and soon the children's screams were echoing through the icy trees surrounding them. They zoomed dangerously close past several dense trunks, and my bellows at Joanna to roll off were cut short when I realized that they were heading straight for a massive pine.

"Oh, my God," Emily cried out and threw her gloved hands over her face. "Please, no."

"Joanna," I yelled, louder than I thought myself capable of. In a second, the front door to the cabin flew open, and there was Ma, wide-eyed with her hand clutched over her swollen belly.

I wondered if we would wipe the vibrant blood splatters from the trees after this terrible accident, or if we'd just let the snow build up over it all until everything was white again. I wondered how I would feel for the rest of my life knowing that my little brother and sister were dead because of me.

But by God's grace, Joanna suddenly rolled off the sled, clutching Charles to her chest as she did. The children tumbled over one another with violent speed, but came to a sudden stop when they collided with a dense cluster of bushes. The snow from the bushes flew away from the branches and scattered quietly around their bodies.

The sled, newly free of its previous weight, veered to the right before crashing into another tree, making a horrific cracking sound and snapping itself clean in half. Shattered bark exploded away from the trunk, and then all was finally still.

Ma's cries were ragged as she stumbled out into the snow, and I only vaguely noted that she wasn't wearing boots. She strode through the white, her dress dragging in a soaked pile behind her, and reached into the bushes to grab Charles.

Emily cried out in relief when Ma set Charles standing upright and he stayed that way. Soon after, Joanna was at his side, shaking like a leaf but with no broken bones or blood. Ma pulled them back into the house, Emily and I trailing wordlessly behind. Once inside, Ma produced four mugs filled to the brim with steaming honey tea. Joanna was still shaking as she drank hers, but Charles was as hyper as if he'd eaten a whole package of Christmas sweets in one sitting.

"That was fun, Ma!" he chirped as Ma stepped out of her soaked dress and layers of long underwear. She carefully laid the clothing in front of the fire and stood, shivering, with a blanket wrapped around her while she waited for them to dry. Her largely swollen belly stuck out from the front of the blanket, and I drank my tea even though all I wanted to do was cry.

"Not for me," she said softly as she bounced up and down on her toes. "You almost gave your ma a heart attack."

"Me, too," Emily said after a loud gulp of tea. "I really thought you were both about to be dead."

"Emily!" I said and shook my head at her. "What a thing to say."

"You thought so, too," she quipped back. "I could tell."

"Enough," Ma said sternly, and everyone quieted.

"The Lord kept you safe, and it's all over now. We will say an extra prayer tonight in thanks of our good health."

She was just wiggling back into her dry clothes when Pa came through the door, home from hunting much earlier than usual. His beard was flecked with snow, and when he pulled his hat off, he sent icy water flying over the table where we sat.

"The storm isn't stopping," Pa said in a deep gruff. "And the mountain is becoming unsafe for travel. It's a good thing we have enough supplies to last us for a good few months. We're not going anywhere for a while, at least."

"Oh, my," Ma said and rushed over to pour Pa some tea. "What a harsh winter this has been."

But it turned out harsh wasn't the weather, and harsh wasn't eating nothing but fried cornmeal cakes for days, and harsh wasn't having to stay inside at all times with three other children and two adults. Harsh was the cough that fell upon Ma only a few days after the sledding incident, innocent enough at first but as persistent and increasingly damaging as the storm outside. Harsh was when Ma became so delirious with fever that she started calling us by different names.

Pa was able to shoot a deer and store the body just outside the front door, embedded in snow and frozen solid until it was time to cook it up, chunk by chunk, in either hot water to make broth for Ma or fried in a pan with gravy and potatoes for stew. Pa hoped that the storm would let up a little bit by the time we needed more meat. Ma's cough deepened into a harsh bark that racked her body from the inside out.

By the time a fortnight had passed, the deer was gone, and the steady downfall had transformed into an angry, nearly horizontal monster of whistling winds and bitter cold that was sharp enough to cut straight to the bone. Ma's fever was still raging by then, and we all knew it wouldn't be good for the baby. A miscarriage was suddenly a very real possibility, as was death.

It carried on for three months.

Three months of changing sheets, soaked yellow with perspiration, and hallucinations and forcing broth made with roots or herbs down Ma's throat. The days bled into each other, and one early evening as Emily went to check on her, she noticed that Ma's water had broken and the time to deliver the baby boy or girl had come.

After Hannah was born, I developed a terrible fear of dying in the winter. Of being buried in a wooden box, six feet beneath a small knob of a headstone, embedded in the frozen ground like a maggot in flesh. I couldn't imagine anything worse than lying there in the dark, wishing for a candle or a blanket or my ma.

Above the ground, things would be silent, except for the icy wind shrieking through the trees of the mountains that would be my final resting place. But below the surface, in the frigid blackness, there'd be sounds.

Squirming. Clawing. Biting. Insects and worms would make their way in, make a nest of the inside of my head, and I'd hear them even more then. I wouldn't be able to scream. I wouldn't be able to fight them off.

How much time will pass before I find myself there? Hannah and my baby were proof that age means nothing, that even the youngest can dance with death before they've had the chance to really live in the first place.

Am I there now?

TWENTY

As soon as it is light out, Emily and I hand out jerky strips to the children for breakfast, then take them outside to sit on the front bench of the wagon while we wait for Pa and Hannah to return. Ma has been waiting inside since dawn came, sitting without a word as she rocks gently in her chair before the fire. Whenever one of us tries to approach her, she waves us off weakly, tells us to keep an eye out for Pa.

The hole in the floor that the ants came up from was tiny, a split in between two boards that was otherwise unnoticeable, but after we saw that the terrible things were gone, we poured hot wax over it to harden anyway.

There are dozens of them still in the dish tub, bloated and shining like red marbles. Most of them were dead last I looked, but some were squirming weakly across the surface of the dirty water in an attempt to cling to the side and each other. I hope they all die slowly.

We sit arm to arm on the wagon bench, with Emily and me on the ends and the children in between us. Nobody speaks. We all concentrate intently on the forest line a mile ahead of us, squinting into the sunlight to search for any sign of life.

I feel as if I should have known something was coming, like the cries in the night were warnings that I did not heed. But how was I meant to prevent the miscarriage, or the ant attack? How was I meant to keep my wits when Hannah transformed into the baby that I saw standing in the prairie that night, with her dead-fish eyes and her ear on my womb, before she nearly flung herself into the fire?

This isn't a test, or a challenge, or a puzzle to be solved and defeated. It's just *happening*.

And it will never stop.

As soon as Pa returns, with or without Hannah, I must do what I can to convince Emily to help me talk to Ma and Pa about leaving the prairie. I will tell them everything, I will tell them about Henry, and the baby, and of the time he told me stories about some haunted fields that sounded a whole lot like the ones Zeke described, a whole lot like *these fields*. I'll bet anything that it was Henry who told my pa about this area in the settlement that day, Henry who drew the map up and eagerly overestimated how many homes would be available just so that Pa would be more likely to leave. That mewling, beef-witted malt worm.

There is one other thing my grandfather always said, Zeke's words repeat suddenly in my mind. *He said that even though the prairie wasn't safe, the forest always would be.*

Dread blooms in my stomach as I imagine something else happening to one of the children or Emily. I must be especially cautious. I don't entirely trust Zeke, but as much as I hate to admit it, we are likely going to need his help.

Midmorning passes in a wave of rolling white clouds and the whistle of winds in the grasses. Birds shriek at one another and play games in the air. The tips of jackrabbit ears can be seen bobbing up and down through the prairie. The forest stays still.

Pa and Hannah still aren't back by midday.

Emily hasn't spoken much since the attack, and neither have the children. What is taking Pa so long? He said he'd come back by morning, even if just alone. Ma has yet to emerge from the cabin, although a few minutes ago I heard her throw another log into the fire. Why does she have a fire going during the day? She must be beside herself over Hannah. I wonder if she even knows what hour it is.

"I'm hungry," Charles pipes up after the sun has started to shift into afternoon. "Can we have some stew?"

"We can't make stew, boil brain!" Joanna says and

crosses her arms. "We don't have a rabbit. Plus, we need to wait until Pa and Hannah return."

"I'll go and get some more jerky," I offer, and stand to stretch my legs. I don't want any of them going into the cabin alone to bother Ma—clearly what she needs right now is space to grieve over what happened. "I'll bring dried apricots, too."

"I don't want any more jerky!" Charles whines, and that's when Joanna turns and slaps him across the face, hard.

Charles's brown eyes widen, and he shrieks in pain, then dissolves into a loud fit of tears so sad and pitiful it nearly takes us all down with it. Emily pulls him to her and tries to soothe him, strokes his hair and glares at Joanna with something so fierce my little sister nearly begins to cry herself.

"Come with me, Jo," I say gently from the ground, and reach to help her jump down.

We walk hand in hand to the cabin. Joanna pulls at her dark curls and tries to conceal her quivering lip. I stop just before the door and kneel down to become eye level with her.

"I know this is scary, Joanna." I tuck her hair behind her ears gently, like Ma does, and she looks at me expectantly with shining eyes. "But we cannot turn on each other, ever. We have to be able to take care of each other, all right? Charles is just worried about Pa."

"I'm sorry, 'Manda." Jo's face crumbles, and she

throws her arms around my neck. "Oh, why aren't they back yet? Pa promised by morning."

I don't know how to answer her. I kiss her temple and her forehead and her hair, then take her hand and lead her into the cabin to get lunch. Ma is still in her chair. She hasn't changed out of the nightgown she was wearing during the attack—it is wrinkled and dotted with dried bloodstains from Hannah. Her hair is wild, a startling difference to her usual carefully twisted bun. It lies in a tangled muss of black curls that stick out from all around her head.

"I love you, Ma," Joanna says hopefully. "I love you so very much."

Ma doesn't respond, doesn't turn around at all, and I hurry my little sister along to help me gather the food. By the time we return with stacks of dried meat and a pouch filled with soft golden apricots, Charles has stopped crying and is now sniffing against Emily's arm.

"I'm so sorry, Charles." Joanna climbs back into the wagon with my help and hugs him as tight as she can. "I love you, brother."

"Well, did you get lunch?" he asks eagerly, and Jo can't help but laugh.

We eat in more silence. When Emily is finished, she leans back and crosses her feet over the front of the wagon.

"Why don't you and Charles go play?" she suggests to Joanna after the children are through eating, as well.

"There's no need for you two to worry yourselves sick, leave that to Amanda and me. We'll let you know if we see them coming."

Joanna nods and takes Charles's hand, and I help the children down from the wagon so they can play tag around the front clearing. The sound of the game provides a welcoming end to the time-slowing silence.

"Do you think it's a good sign that he is taking this long?" Emily asks without shifting her focus from the trees. "Or a bad sign?"

"I don't know," I admit. "I want to say that it's a good sign, since they'd probably be back already if it was as simple as Hannah dying."

"Do you think she's going to die?" Emily asks. "Honestly."

Telling the truth is difficult, mostly because it's the first time I'm fully admitting it to myself.

"I just don't see how she could survive after the condition she was in," I say. "The doctor would have to have some sort of miracle medicine."

While we continue to wait, I mull over the possibility of the forest once again in my mind. Committing to something so unknown doesn't seem like the best idea, especially since nothing ever seems to happen on the prairie during the day and I have no idea how I'd even begin to talk Ma into going with us.

I decide that we should stay put until Pa comes back. If there is still no sign of him by the later afternoon, I will begin to consider going in after him myself while Emily stays to take care of the children.

Please, come back to us, Ma, I think, breathing deeply through my nose. *I do not want to make this decision on my own.*

If I did go, what would I say to Emily? That I don't think we're safe, that I didn't just need rest, that it wasn't me going mad but the land itself? How could I convince her after our talk yesterday?

Hannah! I told Emily during our conversation in the rain that Hannah was in danger. Surely she finds the circumstances of the ant attack strange, at least. I grow just a bit of hope.

Just the thought of Hannah, my sweet baby sister with the dark curls and beautiful gray eyes, is too much to bear. I see her wet, red mouth pull into a grin from being tickled, I see her little eyebrows furrow as she stares blankly forward while exploring a new item or landscape with her sea-star hands.

And now I see her face covered in ants, her mouth, her eyes, everything, and the agonizing pierce of her scream echoes in my head. I put my hand over my mouth to keep from crying out. The children whoop as they chase each other around the wagon.

I prayed for this, oh, my God, I *prayed* for her to die. I am so disgusted with myself I can hardly bear it. I must make it right somehow, or at least give everything I can to try.

Another hour passes without any sign of Pa. I tell Emily that I need to speak to her alone, that it's urgent. Once the children have promised to leave Ma alone, she suggests we take a walk away from the cabin for privacy.

"Just as long as we stay away from the fields behind the cabin," I say. Even in the middle of the day, the area chills me. I cannot wait to get my family away from here.

If they believe me, that is.

TWENTY—ONE

"I do not understand what is happening." Emily breaks the silence of our walk right when we reach the home-made fire pit, halfway between the cabin and the woods. "Why would Pa wait so long to come back?"

I look past the grasses and into the thick trees, much larger and more tightly clustered than the ones in the mountains, and the wind is much louder near them, too.

"I have not the slightest idea," I say, shifting my focus to my sister. "But what I'm wondering is why *nobody* has come. You'd think that as soon as Zeke saw what happened to Hannah, he'd come to talk to us, even if Pa couldn't leave. The doctor's cabin is only two miles away. He cared about you enough to come, Emily."

I look again to the trees. "I wonder if Pa never found his way there."

Emily is frowning and solemn, crouching before the fire pit and poking at it with a stick even though it isn't lit. Her braids are frazzled, and little strands of her dark waves have fallen loose about her face. Still, even when my sister should look terrible, she is beautiful.

"Maybe..." Emily pauses to search wildly in her head for answers. "Maybe Pa took Rocky straight to town. Through the woods."

"For what?" I ask.

"A gravestone."

"I guess that could be true," I say. "But why wouldn't he come for Ma? Surely he understood that not showing up would worry her sick?"

I am getting to feel seriously uneasy about the position of the sun. It's getting late already, and the idea of going alone into the forest to find Pa with dark quickly approaching doesn't settle right in my stomach, no matter how safe Zeke's grandfather swore the trees were. I need to hurry.

"And on top of that," Emily says, "there is still the body to consider."

"What about it?"

"Where is it?" Emily sighs in frustration. "It doesn't make sense. Wouldn't Pa have at least brought Hannah back to begin the burial before she started to rot? Why would he bring her with him to town?"

In truth, the idea of Pa going to town through the forest in the first place, without coming back for any supplies first, is a stretch for me to believe anyway. I don't want to say that, though. I need to be careful with how I speak to her.

"Emily," I say, and she doesn't turn from the fire pit. I must choose the right words, I must make my sister believe me. "Do you remember during our talk yesterday, when I told you that I felt as though Hannah was in danger?"

The wind picks up. The weather has finally started to cool into much more pleasant temperatures than when we first arrived. I wish I could enjoy it, the way we all enjoyed each other as a family over our feast last night. Was that really just last night?

"I do," Emily finally answers. She stands. "I don't know what to think about it. If you knew that this would happen—"

"I didn't," I burst out defensively, and my sister's eyes widen. She almost looks afraid of me. "I mean, I was nervous that something bad might happen, but I didn't know that she'd be...be..."

I can't even continue. I wrap my arms around myself and sit on one of the half logs before the circle of stones. Most of the ashes from our story time with Zeke are still inside. Emily stays where she is.

"I need Pa to get back," she says. "I don't even know what I should do right now."

"What *we* should do," I say in correction. "Come on, Emmy, please. I need you right now. I need you to believe me."

"That the prairie is evil?" Emily cries. She is not convinced; she is angry. "Sister, I can't trust you, I haven't been able to for as long as I can remember, I don't even *want* to know how you knew something bad would happen to Hannah, or why, or what that says about you—"

"You cannot be serious!" I stand now, my heart pounding in my chest. "I thought we were to be dearest friends forever, Emily. How can you say these things to me right now, how can you find it within yourself to blame me for Hannah? I am still your sister!"

Her face softens at my emotion a little. Please, Emily, *please*.

"I'm sorry," she says, and shakes her head back and forth quickly. "No, no, of course I cannot blame you for the ants. I'm just...scared, I think. And very confused. Oh, Amanda." She sinks to sit on the log behind me, and I join her.

"I want to get our family out of here," I say, barely above a whisper. "I want to go into the forest myself and find Pa, while you stay here with the children. And when I come back with him, we all need to leave for Elmwood as soon as possible."

"Let Ma watch the children!" Emily argues. "I can go with you, I want to find Pa, too. Zeke told me how to find his cabin—"

"No," I say firmly, and look over my shoulder to the prairie cabin. Charles and Joanna are tiny flecks against the sky, still running around the front clearing in their game. "I need you to protect the children, sister, and make sure that nothing happens to them. Ma isn't herself, she hasn't been ever since last night, and we can't count on her to take care of them in her grief. I think that the only person able to console her right now is Pa."

What I don't mention is that I am also insistent on going alone because I want to protect Emily from myself as well, and also Zeke, on the chance that he's somehow preventing Pa from returning. The Kensington story is still fresh in my mind, not to mention the fact that I seem to evoke death upon any children that are near. Two gone now, thanks to me. I won't let it happen to the rest of them.

Emily grabs one of her braids and begins to chew the ends as she thinks, a habit that has always made my stomach turn. She considers my idea as her eyes dart around the line of trees that begin the forest.

"All right," she says finally and stands from the log. "But if you don't come back within a few hours, I *will* be coming in after you. I'm trusting you right now, sister. Last time you wanted to go on a walk in the woods by yourself—"

"I know," I say, irritated. I fight the urge to put my hand over my belly. "You don't need to remind me."

She lets out a quick huff of breath. "I said I'd go along with your plan, didn't I?"

"All right, then," I say, and go to hug Emily. "Let us not fight at a time like this." She returns the embrace, but something about her feels stiff, hesitant. It makes me want to cry.

When we get back to the cabin, Joanna and Charles are sitting together on the back of the wagon, their heads bent together as they whisper back and forth with faces far too serious for their age. They look relieved to see us.

"Ma kept asking where you were," Joanna says in a quiet voice. "She kept asking about it, no matter how many times we answered her. She's acting very queerly."

"I think it's best that we all leave Ma alone for now," I say and look to the cabin. Smoke billows from the chimney. "She needs space to process whatever it is that happened."

"Where are Hannah and Pa and Rocky?" Charles cries, and buries his face in his hands. "Why haven't they come back yet?"

"I don't know, Charles," I say. "But I am going to find out."

Emily and I leave the children to their whispering to go check on Ma. She's sitting on the rocking chair, her hands folded neatly in her lap. She looks so dehydrated and exhausted, yet her demeanor is oddly pleasant. When she hears us enter the cabin, her head turns sharply in our direction. Her hair is still down, surrounding her face with kinks of curl.

"Emily," she says and licks her lips. They are dry and cracked, from the heat of the fire maybe. "Amanda."

"Hello, Ma." I approach her slowly, with caution. "How are you feeling?"

"Oh, just fine!" she pulls her flaking lips apart into a smile. "I was just thinking about you. Where did you two go, just now?"

"We went to our fire pit, Ma," Emily says. "Remember how we told you before we left?"

"You did nothing of the sort," Ma hisses suddenly, causing both my sister and I to jump. "Tell me, my loves, did you go to the forest? Tell your sweet Ma the truth."

Emily and I glance at each other in alarm. Ma shrugs to adjust her filthy nightgown.

"The forest?" I say. Her behavior is terrifying to witness. She is not herself; this is not my ma. My heart will not slow down. "Of course we didn't. It's true, what Emily said. We only went to the fire pit."

"Good." Ma leans into the rocking chair, hands folded once more, and rocks back and forth while she stares into the flames. "You are never to go into those trees. Ever."

"Why?" Emily asks gently, and kneels down beside the chair. "Do you know why Pa is taking so long to get back, Ma?"

Ma pauses, and for a moment I think that maybe she's going to ignore my sister. Her eyes shine, dancing with the flames, unblinking, and the smallest hint of a grin flickers upon her face. She suddenly looks over at Emily.

"There's a demon," Ma whispers, her voice hoarse.

She speaks as if someone else is listening, and I have to lean in closer to hear her words.

"A demon in the woods," she whispers again. "We don't want it slithering on its belly over here to *us*, now, do we?"

Emily and I stare openmouthed at this woman with the wild hair and rough voice. I'm dreaming, I think to myself. This is a nightmare. What has happened to my ma? Emily's eyes are growing wet.

"Don't worry, though." Ma turns her gaze back to the fire, her eyes bloodshot from forgetting to blink. "We're safe here, in this prairie. Your pa will be back before you know it."

"What do you mean a d-demon?" I stutter.

Ma stops rocking then. "What was it, Amanda, that I just said? Not one minute ago? It was in the trees."

"I'm...I'm sorry." I stand and take a step back. "We'll leave you alone, Ma."

"Good little children," she sighs and begins to rock again. Her hands curl over each other in her lap. "I need to go fetch some meat for lunch. Your pa wouldn't want us to starve on his account, I'm quite sure."

Ma stands and goes to the corner of the cabin, where she slides on a pair of Pa's work boots. It is far too early to begin preparing supper. Emily is no longer looking at me like I am crazy.

I've only ever seen Ma hunt once, in the mountains when Pa tried teaching her how to shoot. She got a quail after five or six shots, but still swore she'd never use the rifle again unless defending us against a bear. As she stands at the doorway holding it now, with her blood-shot eyes and thin legs stemming out of boots far too large for her and hair matted into dense tangles, she is an eerie sight to behold.

"Goodbye," she sings, and steps outside. "Goodbye, sweet daughters."

Emily and I go outside at once to be near the children.

"I told you something here is amiss," I say under my breath. "Maybe Ma saw something, like I did, or maybe she's hearing things—"

"I will not hear any more talk about demons," Emily cuts me off. "I'm uncomfortable with this enough as it is. Let's just stick to the plan to find Pa. We'd be silly to listen to Ma about the woods being dangerous, Zeke *lives* there, and he specifically told us that they were safe. She's clearly delirious in her grief."

"But you'll help me convince Ma and Pa to leave, right?" I look to my sister in desperation. "After Pa is back? You have to know that we aren't safe here."

"I'll help you," Emily confirms, expressionless, and I breathe a sigh of relief. "As soon as lunch is through, you should head out to Zeke's cabin."

TWENTY—TWO

"We need to talk about Ma."

"I know!" Charles pipes up, climbing to sit on the fence beside Emily. "I think something funny happened to her because she misses Pa and Hannah. I find myself to be afraid of her!"

"I understand it," I say, and Emily nods. "But you have no reason to worry. After lunch is through, I will be going on Blackjack to find Pa."

"Thank the Lord." Jo sighs and sits next to me.

"Still," Emily adds, "it's very important to let Ma be for right now. Don't ask her any questions, only speak when spoken to, and always stay very close to me."

"Will Ma strike us, do you think?" Joanna wonders.

"She will do nothing of the sort," I say. "If you feel afraid, we can come up with a secret way to show it so that you can tell Emily or me without alarming Ma. I don't think she's violent, I think she's just very, very upset about what happened to Hannah." *Or being driven mad by infant cries that nobody else can hear,* I think. "We mustn't upset her further."

"Is Hannah dead?" Charles asks.

Nobody says anything for a while. Joanna kicks at the swaying prairie grass with her boot.

"If I must be honest, little ones—" my voice is shaking "—I think that perhaps she is. I don't know this for sure. It's just what I believe."

"I thought so," Joanna says, but begins to cry anyway.

It doesn't take long for Charles to follow suit. Emily and I hug the children close while they wail into our sleeves.

"She's with our Lord now," Emily whispers through her own tears into Charles's hair. "She's happy in Heaven, listening to the songs of angels and basking in the warmth of the eternal light."

I shut my eyes and picture it, a happy Hannah with wings, with no more confusion or frustration. I imagine her sitting on a fluffy cloud, giggling and clapping her hands in joy. My last image of her stains the vision, makes it drip with black, prairie ants lodged in her nose and ears and mouth.

From the distance comes a gunshot, then another, then another. Ma must have gotten her rabbit.

"What should our code be?" Joanna sniffs after their cries fade into hiccups. "To let you and Emily know that we're scared?"

"I know!" Charles speaks up. "We should say, 'grass-hopper bait.'"

"I think she'd figure out that something funny was going on," Emily says with a half grin. "We need something a little more subtle."

"How about a tune?" I suggest. "You could hum a certain tune, and we'd know that you're afraid."

"Good idea," Emily says. "Now, what tune should we use?"

I think about the last time I held Hannah and hummed with her face against my chest, and my breath catches.

"How about 'Come, Holy Ghost'?" I suggest. "I always liked that one."

"Oh, me, too," Joanna exclaims. "It really is lovely."

"Very well," Emily says, then hops down from the fence. "That settles it, then. Try not to use it too often, though, or she'll catch on."

"Amanda?" Joanna asks. From the distance we can see Ma, shuffling through the grass back toward the cabin. "Does Ma still love us?"

"Of course," I say and squeeze her hand. "And Pa does, too."

"I can't wait to see Pa again," Charles sighs.

"Trust me," Emily says to the children and kicks at a rock. "Neither can we."

"I'll call you when the feast is ready!" Ma yells at us from the cabin door, waving with her free hand. The

rifle is tucked under her arm, and there is a large bulging sack grasped in her hand. She disappears into the
cabin.

We wait for what feels like an hour. Smoke billows
from the chimney on the roof of the cabin, and with
each minute I grow more and more impatient. I'm
about to suggest to Emily that I leave before the food is
ready when Ma pokes her head out from the front door
and yells at us to come join her immediately. We all go
together as I try to think of ways to sneak off without
alerting attention to myself.

The cabin smells funny, unfamiliar, meaty but not
like stew or fried meat strips. A dead rabbit lies carved
apart in a bowl in the corner, and beside it lie two others that are untouched besides the bullet wounds in
their heads or chests. Their blood seeps down through
the fluffy white fur, staining the new hardwood floor.

We each sit before an empty plate in the circle Ma has
arranged in the middle of the floor. Nobody asks what
we are having to eat.

"Here it is," Ma sings and pulls a dish from the fire
with heavy pads. "A pie for my lovelies."

"Pie?" Joanna says and licks her lips.

"Yes." Ma sets the dish down before us. She kneels
before it, knife in hand, and I find myself anxious at
the sight. "Dried apple pie."

Apple? I know for a fact that Pa didn't get any dried
apples on his last supply purchase, and the smell in the

air is that of anything but fruit. Emily bites her lower lip and studies the pie.

It's a pie, there's no denying it, covered in a vented layer of cornmeal dough that is slightly burnt around the edges. Ma shoves the tip of the knife into the pie and begins to saw away.

"First piece for the baby," she says and grabs Charles's plate. She plops a huge piece on to it, then slides it back in front of him.

The pie is filled with something lumpy and gray. The gravy runs clear in places and cloudy in others. The smell makes my stomach turn as easily as if I'm still with child.

"Eat up, my littlest," Ma encourages Charles. Emily and I look at each other in wonder. Ma finishes filling the rest of our plates with the steaming pie.

"Why is nobody eating?" Ma asks when she notices our stares. Her enthusiasm dies, and her dark eyebrows pull together in the center. "Eat it. Now."

"Are you..." I clear my throat, afraid to set her off. "Are you sure this is apple, Ma?"

"You ungrateful bitch," Ma snaps in my face, knife still in hand, and the children's eyes widen in horror. She points the knife toward my face. "Now, I really must insist that you try it. You'll never know if you like it, unless."

My heart is pounding in my throat. The knife is still pointed to me. I take my fork with a shaking hand and gather a bite of the stinking pie. A large, dark slimy thing falls from the fork and lands on the plate, and I study it in disgusted curiosity.

"That's probably the liver," Ma says. "Or the heart. You really don't want to miss either of them, regardless. Eat it, lovey."

Charles begins to hum "Come, Holy Ghost," and Joanna joins in almost instantly. No matter how subtle the song choice, the timing is terrible. Ma's eyes flash to the children, narrowed with confusion.

"It's singing time now, is it?" she asks. "Well, I can see that nobody is hungry."

She makes a quick movement for me all of the sudden, from across the floor, and for an instant I think she is going to drive the knife right into my eye or my stomach or my throat. But instead the fork in my hand is snatched away. The remaining food on it flies over the floor and Ma's lap.

"Ungrateful children don't get lunch," she says and spears another rabbit organ from the pie. She shoves it into her mouth and chews viciously, and I can hear the gristle grinding like sand between her teeth. Fluid dribbles from her smacking lips and down her chin. "Or dinner, or breakfast. In fact, I think that none of you will ever eat anything, ever again."

I cannot leave them here when I go, I realize. *She is going to kill us all.*

Emily stands up and motions for Jo and Charles to do

the same. They do and move behind Emily. "We're going to go play, Ma," Emily says and starts leading them out.

Wait, you're leaving me, I want to cry out, but my legs won't work and I can't stand up and the children need to be taken away. I understand why Emily is abandoning me, but that does nothing to ease the panic.

"I don't want to see your faces back in this cabin again," Ma yells at them. Tears well up in Charles's brown eyes. "You can live outside like the little animals that you are."

They leave, and I'm left sitting on the floor to watch my ma attempt another bite of the gizzard pie. After three chews, she vomits into the pie dish, filling it back to the brim. I finally find the strength to stand and back away when she starts eating at it just as eagerly as before.

"I'm...going to go join the children," I say, struggling not to scream, struggling not to run. She looks up at me through yellowed eyes, and my heart skips a beat.

"It's you," Ma says, as if seeing me for the first time. "The one who wouldn't let me in when I knocked. I didn't think it was possible, but this one had just as much guilt as you did. Delicious."

I take another step back. "Wouldn't let you in?"

"I tried and tried, but in the end there was no room for me, oh, no." She stops eating for a moment, tilts her head curiously. "Because you already *have* a devil in you, girl. I see him whispering in your ear right now."

Sinner.

I cannot move. I must get to the door, and I cannot move.

"You prayed for those babies to die," she rasps now, much louder than before, her voice completely changed. "You prayed for those babies to die and *yet you wonder* what it is that is wrong with you?"

I feel very light-headed all of a sudden, as if I am going to faint, and the thing that calls itself my ma continues to stuff its face, without a care that the pie is spilling onto the front of the already stained nightdress.

"Your little bastard would have been a girl, you know," it adds through a full mouth. "Dark hair, just like her ma, with the nose of her father. Giggly like Joanna, and smart like Emily. And, Amanda—" it pauses swiftly to take another bite "—she would have *hated your guts.*"

Her body shudders then, and whatever this creature is clears my ma's throat and lifts a single eye to stare into my soul. "That wasn't me who collected your baby's slime into my earth," it finishes. "Oh, no, deary, that was God."

I back away another two steps and nearly trip over my own feet. Ma grins up at me, her teeth clotted with dark liquid.

"You fucked that boy in the mountains," it says and begins to giggle hysterically. "*But there was no baby! There was no baby! There was no—*"

I turn and sprint from the cabin, and the laugh that

chases me out sounds like it is made up of many voices, and I fight with all my might not to faint. After I slam the door behind me, I trip over my own feet and come facedown in the grass. I'm convinced that she's going to emerge from the cabin any second, her chin and neck shining with gravy, ready to use the pie pan to crack my head open like a hen's egg.

I wait, but the cabin door stays closed. Emily rushes to my side in alarm.

"What happened, sister?" she asks and pulls me up. "Are you all right? You're soaked through with sweat! Did she hold the knife to you again?"

It all comes together, then. Zeke's story of Jasper Kensington murdering his family. A cabin found stinking with blood before it was rebuilt and claimed by our family. Henry telling me about ruined flatlands that could come out to play through the living if it wanted.

The one who wouldn't let me in when I knocked, the Ma-thing said to me just now. *You already have a devil in you, girl.*

The devil in the woods has been here all along.

The prairie tried to possess me at first, pulling me in with cries in the dark and an infant standing in the grass, and when it found that my soul was already claimed, it got angry, it came out to play through Ma and a swarm of fire ants instead.

"We need to leave," I stammer as my body shakes. "That man Zeke told us about, Kensington, we're living in his cabin, it's going to happen to Ma if we stay. We need to bring the children with us, it's not safe here, we have to get away right this very instant—"

"I...I believe you," Emily says. The color in her face has drained. "I really do, Amanda. That wasn't Ma in there, oh, my word, that wasn't Ma at all. Zeke said the forest would be safe, like you mentioned, he must have known something. Why didn't he just *tell us*?"

I notice for the first time that Joanna and Charles are staring at me, openmouthed, from the back of the wagon. Their faces are aghast with fear.

"Everything will be all right," I promise them, for what is one more lie after all that I've told? "But it's time to go now, children."

They jump down from the wagon and follow us eagerly to where Blackjack is grazing.

"Are we going to find Pa now?" Charles whimpers.

"Yes," I say, and the children sigh in relief. "We are."

TWENTY—THREE

"No matter what happens," Emily tells the children for the tenth time, "do not come out of this spot for any reason, whatsoever. You wait here until we come and get you, do you understand?"

We are all gathered around an enormous hollowed log whose end is hidden by a large, leafy bush. The children are crouched inside, their heads together, their arms wrapped around each other. Both of them have tears in their eyes.

"Very well," Joanna whimpers. "Just, please, hurry, sisters."

After putting the children on Blackjack and leading the horse to the start of the trees, Emily and I argued about what to do next for minutes, neither of us tearing our eyes away from the cabin in the distance in case Ma started to come after us. When she continued to stay inside, we broke through the barrier and delved deeper into the forest. With no horse, it would take Ma at least an hour to find the spot, if she decided to come looking. We had to act quickly.

Emily originally wanted to bring the children with us to Zeke's cabin, but I was insistent about the possibility of there being danger waiting for us. If something happened and we had to go quickly, we'd be stuck since there is only one horse between the four of us. Even if we all piled on, any speed faster than a walk could send us flying to crack open our heads on the ground below.

Well, what do we do then? Emily cried out in frustration. *We certainly can't send them back to the prairie. And I'm not letting you go alone with Blackjack.*

After some more deliberation, I had an idea: we could hide the children, go look for Pa, and hopefully bring him back to retrieve Joanna and Charles before heading into Elmwood. If we couldn't find Pa by the time night was falling, we'd take the children to the settlement ourselves, by the light of the moon where the fields meet the trees. I don't know what else we could possibly do.

"I don't think that Ma will be able to come into the forest," I assured the children after we found the perfect hiding place. "It should be safe here."

Then, where is Pa?

We have no choice. After warning them once again to stay put and stay quiet, Emily lets the bush fall back into place. The children are completely hidden from view. I memorize the spot in my mind, burn it in, *do not forget this tree.* We mount Blackjack, me in front, Emily behind me, and keep heading deeper in the opposite direction of the prairie.

The forest in the mountains was hardly ever quiet, except in the dead of winter, and usually buzzed with the sound of animals and insects that could always be heard in the air.

Here, there is no sound. We see a single deer as we ride through, small with alarmed eyes and brown spotted fur, and the second it sees us, it bolts away and disappears in four swift prances. Blackjack picks up his pace without being prompted.

I imagine the children lying in the bushes, wrapped around each other and shaking with fright, and my throat closes.

"They're safe for now," Emily says as if reading my mind. "But we do need to make this quick, Amanda."

After we've ridden for another half mile or so, I halt the horse, and Emily glances all around us.

"Didn't you say it was supposed to be straight out from where Zeke usually rode through?" I say with uncertainty. "I don't see anything."

"I don't either," Emily says, leaning to the side as if straining to hear. "Hush!"

I quiet myself and turn to watch Emily. She lifts her hair away from her ears and leans even farther. "Do you hear that?" she murmurs quietly.

I strain my ears. "No," I start to say, but then I *do* hear something. It's very far off, very faint, a high-pitched tone that sounds exactly like screaming children. It's not coming from behind us, thank goodness, at least there's that.

"What on earth is that?" I ask Emily. She shushes me once more.

Blackjack's ears flick and turn themselves to the left. "I think it's coming from the east," my sister says slowly. "It sounds like animals, or something."

"I guess we should go toward it," I say. "It's our only sign so far. Did Zeke ever mention any animals?"

"No, but it's not as if we told each other the stories of our lives," Emily said.

I turn Blackjack to the left, and we weave through the trunks. There are more logs to maneuver over this way, more boulders and ponds to go around. The screaming becomes louder, and Blackjack begins to shudder and cry out.

We only ride for a short time when I see it: the shape of a wide, low cabin, tucked away behind the trees ahead. Emily sees it at the same time as me. Blackjack begins to spook from the sounds of the screaming, growing louder still, and with them the air has grown thick with dread. He rears, threatening to bolt, and I call back for Emily to get down. Once she's off, I lead the horse back a bit until he calms, then secure his reins to a low-hanging branch.

"We'll need to leave him here," I say and hop down

to join Emily. "He won't go any farther. We just need to be careful. Remember this spot, all right?"

Emily nods, slowly. My stomach turns at the feel of the unfamiliar ground beneath my feet.

"All right, sister," I say, and hug Emily in an act of pure nerves. "Let's go."

TWENTY-FOUR

The screams tear over each other, becoming steadily louder as we make our way to the cabin. When we are close enough to smell the smoke coming from the chimney, we begin to duck behind trees. I cannot imagine what I'm about to witness—an animal being slaughtered? Children in agony? I have no other idea as to what could be causing such a terrible noise.

When we're close to the cabin, a large wooden fence comes into view, big and sturdy, that wraps around the entire back end of the dwelling. The high-pitched shrills are coming from inside.

There is no sign of Pa, or Rocky, or Zeke, or Doctor Jacobson anywhere.

"We need to move around," Emily whispers. "We can't see anything from here."

So we dart from tree to tree carefully, quietly, as if playing hide-and-seek on the mountain with the children. My heart aches to return to them. When we've reached the opposite end of the cabin, we cautiously approach the fence, crouching and crawling in the soft moist soil that is riddled with pebbles and sticks and pine needles, so that we would not be visible from inside the house.

My sister and I lower our eyes to a gap in the fence and hold our breath.

Before I know what's happening, our noses are nearly bitten off by a giant swine, the largest I've ever seen, with a fanged mouth that covers the entirety of the gap in the fence. It cries out in anger when we both get away, a frenzied squeal that sounds just like the many coming from behind it.

"Pigs," Emily sighs in relief. "It's only pigs. I thought... I thought that somebody..."

"I know," I say and crawl on my knees to the far corner of the fence for a better look. "So did I." Emily follows, the color drained from her face.

I rise a couple of inches, then a couple more, until I am crouching at the top of the fence and can see down into the pen, as well as the cabin behind it. The cabin is very nice, large with a pointed roof, built with double paned glass windows that Ma would have gone green with envy over. The thought of Ma brings tears to my eyes, but then I see something embedded in the center of the pig pen, bloody and filthy and covered in mud and pig waste.

Hannah's nightgown. And next to it, flattened to almost nothing beneath massive hooves the size of clubs, Pa's hat.

A white jawbone sits gleaming in the dirt by the hat, a row of cracked yellow teeth embedded in a line across the top. I know as soon as I see it that it once belonged to Pa. Before I can react, Emily screams. It blends right into the sound of the pigs.

I didn't even notice that she was standing, too, peeking over the top of the fence with me, and my hand flies over her face in attempt to stop her from making any more sound. We sink to our knees behind the fence, both of us gasping for air, and the pigs seem to scream even louder.

"We need to run," I whisper as soon as I can gather myself enough to do so. "We need to run and get the children *now*."

"How is this happening?" Emily cries, her breath quickening. "What happened to them? I don't understand. What about Zeke..."

"I'm sorry." I can hardly hold myself together as we crawl back through the dirt, covering our skirts with mud. The fence shakes as the pigs run into the other side of it. From the forest ahead of us, I can hear Blackjack crying out in panic. "This is all my fault, I'm sorry for everything, Emily. Oh, my God—"

"The children," Emily repeats as we reach the end of the fence. "We need to get Joanna and Charles."

It's so dim in the forest that it's hard to tell what time

it is or how much light is left out in the prairie. There were clouds rolling in on our way here, I remember, and traveling to Elmwood without the full light of the moon will be extremely difficult. Emily and I prepare to run across the small clearing to the nearest tree large enough to hide behind.

"On the count of three," Emily says and gathers her skirts up around her waist. I do the same.

"One," I whisper.

"Two..."

"Three!" someone behind us yells, someone behind the fence, someone at the back of the cabin. The voice is deep, loud, almost like a *growl*, and cuts over the squeals of the pigs with ease. "Run, girls! *You don't want to be late getting home tonight!*"

We stand to run. I can't help but look back to see who or what is behind me.

It's Doctor Jacobson. And, standing beside him is Zeke.

At least, I think it's Zeke. His face is tinged deep with green and striped with ugly veins that are so dark they look black. He is grinning through his cracked lips, a grin so wide it could be drunk, and the teeth beneath are broken to pieces. The cracked flesh of his mouth bleeds down, smearing the front of his chin with red, and he waves. His hair sticks out in random patches over his head, the majority of it fallen or pulled from the scalp. Emily gasps.

Still beside Zeke is Doctor Jacobson. His glasses are askew, his usually friendly face is unsmiling, and his bald head is speckled with blood and bits of mud. His eyes are open, but he doesn't appear to be here at all.

"Remarkable child she was, Hannah," he calls out to us, and his voice sounds as grated and crumbled as Zeke's. "But I do wish your pa hadn't brought her over here. He spread the infection over the barrier, you see, and already it's changing its ways in the different terrain, already it has adapted to the spirit of the forest. My son wasn't able to stop it this time, *hmm*, Ezekiel?"

Zeke begins to laugh so hard that he coughs on whatever thickness is clogging his throat. The green of his skin, the *rot* of it, is sickening. The patches of missing hair and scarlet grin make him unrecognizable, a monster, yet he stands as though he is in control of himself. *The evil works differently here than it does on the prairie*, I realize with horror. *Anything could happen here.*

"All that time patrolling the forest line to keep the demons out," Doctor Jacobson continues. "I did it myself until Zeke came of age to handle the shotgun. I thought nothing could get his guard down after hearing about what happened to his grandfather after the Kensington incident."

I knew it. Ma has become possessed, just the same as Jasper Kensington. My heart sinks into my stomach.

The doctor sighs. "I should have known he was lying

when he swore the girl wouldn't distract him from his responsibility."

Emily cries out, her eyes brimming with tears. Zeke *was* trying to protect her.

"Like a fool, I went along with his request to let you all live until things got out of hand. Your pa is the one who made the final mistake, though." Doctor Jacobson looks into the pen. "He should have accepted that the baby didn't have a chance after the ant attack. The prairie had claimed that little body, mmm-hmm, and it started to come alive again just minutes after he arrived, but rest assured, girls, that was not Hannah in there, oh, no, *not at all*."

He looks to his son. "We don't stand a chance, Zeke and I. He's almost gone already. Look at him, there isn't any hope for us now..."

"No," Emily wails. My heart is in my throat as I try not to look at the tiny nightgown and half-crushed jawbone in the stinking mud of the pen.

"We fed them both to the pigs, you know," the doctor calls sadly, and he and Zeke climb up so that they are standing over the squealing animals. "We thought it might help. But it was too late. The barrier has been crossed. It isn't just the prairie, anymore, I'm afraid."

Without another word, both Doctor Jacobson and Zeke spread their arms out and fall silently into the pig pen. I hear them both land in the dirt, loud solid *thunks* that spark a frenzied reaction from the swine. Over the ruckus of the screaming animals comes the crunch of snapping bones, the rip of tearing flesh, the popping of snapped cartilage.

The Jacobsons are being eaten alive, but neither of them make a sound.

"Run!" Emily screams and bolts.

I follow her as fast as I can. We sprint through the woods, toward Blackjack's whimpers, jumping over logs and stones and vines and dips. Finally we reach the horse. He's frantic, rearing on his back legs and trying to pull away from the branch. Emily unties it with hands shaking so badly I don't think she'll ever get it.

Finally she does, and in an instant we are up and riding north to the prairie, the horse moving with frightened precision and a clear memory of how to get out. Emily tightens her arms around my middle, crying into my back.

There's no doubt about it now—Ma is never coming back. All that remains of the Verner family are Emily and me and the children. And our cabin, or the land that the Kensington cabin sits on, has been evil all along. Did Henry know this would happen when he drew the map out for my pa and sent our family into Hell?

The Jacobsons' cabin falls farther and farther away every time I look back, and then I can't see it anymore at all. I lead Blackjack to the tree I burned into my mind, the tree that marks where we hid the children, frantic, crying out their names over and over again.

There comes no answer.

I nearly leap from the top of the horse, and Emily stays on, to keep control of Blackjack and make sure he doesn't bolt. I tear the bush back from the hollowed log, tears streaming down my face.

The children are gone.

TWENTY-FIVE

"We promised we'd protect them," Emily says through her tears. "We failed them, Amanda, our own brother and sister."

"They're still alive," I insist, frantic, as we peer at the prairie cabin from the edge of the forest. "I know it. They have to be. We have to get them."

The sun is low, but still high enough to lend us light for at least some of the ride to Elmwood. "If the children are alive and we can manage to harness the ox to the wagon—"

"Why did we ever leave our mountain?" Emily whispers behind me. "We're all going to die here."

"You mustn't talk like that," I scold. "What if we just rode close enough to look through the window?" I ask, and nudge Blackjack forward through the grass. "I can see if they're alive or not, and if we need to bolt, we can."

Let them be alive, I beg. *Please.*

"Oh, I can't bear the thought of any more death,

Amanda," Emily says. "But I feel as though it is inevitable."

"No, Emily," I argue. "Have faith, sister, I will take us away from here, and the children, as well."

We're about halfway to the cabin when we both hear it, a sliding note of music with the sweet woody sound that can only be made by Pa's fiddle. Someone inside the cabin is playing a flawless version of "Come, Holy Ghost." And with the tune blends the voices of Joanna and Charles, high-pitched and shaking, and my arms break out into gooseflesh.

Come, Holy Ghost, Creator blest,
And in our souls take up your rest;
Come with your grace and heavenly aid
To fill the hearts which you have made.

O Comforter, to you we cry,
O heavenly gift of God Most High,
O fount of life and fire of love,
And sweet anointing from above.

You in your sevenfold gifts are known;
You, finger of God's hand we own;
You, promise of the Father, you
Who do the tongue with power imbue.

"I told you they're alive!" I cry out, thankful beyond words at the second chance. "I won't let her have them, Emily. We will not fail them again."

"Yes," my sister says. "I hope you're right, Amanda."

The song is nearly through when we break into the front yard of the cabin. Smoke billows from the chimney, and the fiddle plays on without skipping a beat. The only thing that keeps me moving forward is the voices of my siblings.

I will do whatever it takes to get them back, I promise myself. *That thing is not my ma. I will kill it if I must.*

"I need you here with me," I say to Emily, and she nods sharply. "Can you focus? Are you ready?"

"Yes," she whispers, and her hands curl into fists. "Let's just get them and get out of here."

Without a word, my sister and I stalk to the front door, ready to scream at the children to run to us, and I put my hand on the doorknob.

"Come in," calls Ma's voice, twisted into something different, before I even turn the knob.

I push the door open, ready for anything.

Wrong.

I am only vaguely aware that the brand-new hardwood floor is completely ruined with blood. It puddles in large pools, all around, not leaving a corner untouched. It's splattered over the mattresses, the newly shaved walls, and drips over the front of Ma's naked body as she sits rocking in her chair. She is wearing the grizzly-bear rug over herself like a coat, and jerkily plays Pa's fiddle with perfect precision.

In the center of the floor is the head of Peter, the ox.

"Help us, Amanda!" Joanna cries from the back corner, where she sits with Charles in her arms. "She's going to eat us!"

The fiddle music stops midnote. I dash to the side of the door, where Pa's hunting knife is lying, bloodied, on the floor. The demon sets the fiddle down gently and stands to face us.

"Do you have it in you, girl?" it says to me through my ma's mouth. "Do you have what it takes to kill your ma? She blamed you for last winter, you know. She was humiliated by the weakness of your mind, after she fought so hard, for so long, to keep this heart beating..."

"Be quiet!" Emily yells at the demon. "It's lying, Amanda, of *course* it's lying. It's toying with you. Don't be distracted now—"

I squeeze my fist around the warm, slippery handle of the knife even harder to try and get my hand to stop shaking. Do I even have a chance against this thing? If I move for it, will it catch my wrist in its hand, break my arm from the socket, bake my insides into a pie?

"Distractions!" Ma hisses. "Amanda Verner loves distractions, oh, yes. She'll get them however she can, by a clawed creature in the woods, by a post boy writhing on the forest floor, by pretending that she was capable of protecting poor little Hannah..."

"Don't you speak her name!" I step toward the demon, and the children scream. It doesn't move a muscle; in fact, it looks amused, still naked and covered in blood and cloaked with the grizzly-bear rug. *Do something*, my mind screams, and I throw a weak slice with the blade across the creature's forearm. My ma's skin opens, but only just a little; it's too shallow a cut to inflict any real damage.

"Oh, *Hannaaaaah*," the demon sings, and I am momentarily distracted by the sudden movement on the ground.

The ants have returned.

They cover my boots, try to make their way up my legs, frenzied, *fast*, faster even than the ones that got my baby sister. I back away in time to avoid them for the most part, and just as I feel the first bite on my thigh, I hear the children scream. The ants are making their way for Joanna and Charles, who stand and back up into the corner of the cabin.

"Move across the room!" I yell, not taking my eyes from the demon, holding the knife up once again. "I won't let it come after you. Get away from the ants!"

The children run over the frantic layer of prairie ants, their boots making slick crunching noises as they make their way to Emily.

"Oh, you won't, won't you?" The demon steps forward and grabs my throat. I feel my windpipe being crushed beneath the tremendous strength of my ma's arm as I'm lifted completely off the ground. An ant bite comes alive with pain on my stomach, then my hip, then my thigh again. "I knew from the first moment I sensed you on my earth that you were completely pathetic."

I've ruined everything, I think as my vision begins to blur. *I've made my last mistake...*

Suddenly we're knocked off balance, and the creature drops me to the floor. I move away from the ants, gasping for air, and realize that Emily has knocked the demon over. My sister sits on her knees, cradling the side of her head with her hands. The demon stands, and the grizzly rug falls off.

Most of the hair from my ma's head has been torn out, and some of the raw patches on her scalp are shining with blood and pus. "I will kill you now," the demon spits at my sister, truly angry for the first time. "No more toying."

No.

"Come and give your ma a kiss," it snarls, and lunges for Emily. She screams.

Before I know what I'm doing, I've run up to the thing and sunk the hunting blade deep into its temple. It blinks, blabbering nonsense, and stumbles backward. The ants stop moving, stop biting, start receding through the cracks and holes on the ground they came from.

Emily makes a dash for the front door with the children. "Come on, sister!" she cries. "Come *on!*"

The demon snarls and throws Ma's hand at me,

weakly. "Sinner," it says, and lets out a grated giggle. "You'll always...be...a..."

With a guttural cry, I lower my shoulder and charge the abomination. We collide, and I shove it backward into the mouth of the roaring fireplace.

The demon is still screaming by the time we harness Blackjack up to the wagon and load the children inside. The smoky smell of roasting meat fills the air, and I become sick into the grass. By the time we are heading steadily away from the cabin by the light of the late afternoon sun, the children sleeping on top of one another and Emily at my side on the bench, the screams have finally died away like a dissolving nightmare.

TWENTY—SIX

"Elmwood is so far away," Emily says in a low voice as the wagon bumps through the prairie. The sun is falling lower and lower with every minute, and neither of us have any idea of what we should do. "I don't quite know how I feel about going there instead of back to the mountain. It's getting late, and the light of the moon is going to be blocked by those clouds. We'd have to camp."

"We will have to camp anyway, for Blackjack." I throw a glance behind my shoulder into the back of the wagon. Joanna and Charles are sleeping, their arms wrapped around each other, their faces set in frowns even in slumber. At least they are alive. "But either way, sister, we are going to need supplies. The only thing we have is the barrel of water that Pa filled the afternoon before Hannah got attacked."

Without all the added weight of the family's belongings, the mostly empty wagon is able to glide through the tall grasses much more quickly than on the way here. I'd like to get as far away as possible before we are forced to stop to let the horse rest. The closer we can get to Elmwood, to other people and supplies and help, the better, but I know from Pa's experience that the trip could potentially take us a full day's worth of time since we aren't completely sure where it is.

"I've just thought of something," Emily says, and straightens her back. "Do you remember that cabin we passed on the way in to the Kensington place, with the children waving to us from the fence?

I can't believe I'd forgotten. There had been a cabin on the way here, somewhere far away from the tree line, and at the time we'd all been so upset to discover that it was occupied.

"Perhaps we could make our way there to get help!" I say. "Do you think they'd give us supplies?"

"It's worth a try," Emily says. "At the very least, it's on the way to the mountain."

And so we have a plan. We ride for a long time in silence, and I wonder if Emily's mind is having just as hard of a time digesting all of this as mine is. I am plagued by flashbacks of the earlier days on the prairie, of discovering the ruined cabin, of hearing an infant crying in the night, of feeling the hand on my wrist.

Of losing my baby.

That wasn't me who collected your baby's slime into my

earth. The demon's words repeat in my head, just as unwaveringly cruel as they were the first time I heard them back at the cabin. *Oh, no, deary, that was God.*

I prayed for no more baby.

Sinner.

I prayed for no more Hannah.

You already have *a devil in you, girl.*

"Stop the wagon," I say, suddenly unable to sit still. "You need to leave me here, you need to go on without me..."

"What?" Emily looks at me in shock, the corners of her mouth beginning to pull back in panic. "What are you talking about, sister?"

"I'm evil," I say, and I break out into a cold sweat. "The demon in the woods has been inside of me all along. Don't you remember what that thing inside of Ma said to me? It couldn't get in, Emily!"

"It couldn't get in because *you wouldn't let it in*," Emily emphasizes, refusing to slow Blackjack down. "Because you're an especially strong person."

"If you only knew how weak I am!" I burst, and Joanna startles awake for a moment before falling back into uneasy snores. "If you only knew what thoughts have run through my head, Emily, if you only *knew* how despicable, how disgusting, how positively—"

"What are you saying?" Emily cuts me off. "It doesn't matter what you think, sister. It matters what you *do.*

If we were to be damned for every thought that ran through our minds, we'd all be Hell-bound. What matters is who you are."

"And who am I, Emily?" I have no more tears to shed; I only feel dead inside.

"You are stronger than you think you are," Emily says. "You are not your thoughts. The only devil inside of you is the one you created yourself."

I say nothing. Is it possible that she's right?

"I refuse to leave you behind," she continues. "I refuse to let you give up on yourself again. Have you forgotten about what you did just now? *You* stabbed the demon. *You* pushed it into the fire, even though you knew you could have died doing so."

"I had to, though." I shudder at the memory of Ma's face as it twisted in pain in reaction to the knife and the flames. "I had to protect you, and the children..."

"And there it is," Emily says. "That is who you are. You are someone who would risk your life to protect the people that you love. You are someone who makes mistakes, just like everybody else."

The sky deepens to a soft purple-red as the sun finally sinks into the horizon. Ever since the mountain I have felt an unspoken gap between Emily and me, a total lack of understanding, a loss of sisterhood that I feared could never be regained. And now as I look into the face of my younger sister who should have been my older sister, I realize that it was I, once again, who has misunderstood.

She will always be here for me, and I for her. That's the most important thing, now that our ma and pa and Hannah have been taken away from us. The pain of it all is deeper than I could have ever imagined, but we are not alone. We must take care of each other now, always, and the children, as well.

"Thank you, Emily," I say, and move over enough to wrap her in a hug. Despite all we've been through and how truly exhausted she looks, my sister smiles at the embrace and leans into it. "I love you."

"And I you."

That's when we see it at the same time: the cabin we passed on the way to finding our new homestead. It lies just ahead in a spot that is miles from the tree line.

"That's it!" Emily says. "I'm sure of it. Oh, I hope they'll give us supplies. I'm not sure if our foraging skills from the mountains will be of much use here, at least until we get farther away from the flatlands."

She quickly flicks the reins up, then down, and Blackjack speeds up a little at the sight of a sure destination.

"Let's not wake the children," I say when we're close. "They need all the rest they can possibly get."

"Are we going to tell the owners of the cabin what happened?" Emily asks as the wagon draws nearer. Her mouth pulls to the side. "If we do, there's a very good chance they'll turn us away out of fright."

"Agreed," I say. "All we need to reveal is that we've lost our ma and pa and need any help they can offer. If they ask, say it was a sickness."

Emily's eyes grow misty. "It was sick, all right."

As we get closer to the cabin, we are greeted with a strange sight. Just as there were when we passed by the first time, there are three small children sitting on the fence outside of the house, waving to us. Even after we return the gesture, the waving doesn't stop.

"Is this striking you as peculiar?" Emily asks as she leans forward and squints at the children. "Kind of an odd time to be playing outside, in the beginnings of the night. And why won't they stop waving?"

My stomach sinks more with every rotation of the wagon wheel. The children still have not stopped waving. The outlines of their bodies look increasingly funny as we draw nearer—out of proportion, strangely tall but with tiny heads. "Don't stop the horse when we're near," I instruct. "Let me try to call out to them from the wagon first."

But as soon as we're close enough to make out the truth, Emily jolts the reins and makes Blackjack speed away from the cabin. For each of the three children, who sat waving to us from atop the fence with such enthusiasm, aren't actually children at all, nor are they sitting on the fence, like we thought.

They're scarecrows, posted *behind* the fence, all three in a perfectly straight row. *Henry told me about these once,* I realize as I stifle the urge to vomit. Did he know they were real when he told me the story? Did he know exactly where he was sending us that day he recommended the prairie to Pa? I vow to ask him myself one day.

For instead of having straw-filled burlap sacks for heads, these scarecrows have been given *real* heads, sewn on at the neck with thick black cord, heads that once belonged to children. They don't stop waving, their gloved hands floating back and forth in hurried excitement. In their free hands are pieces of someone; an arm, a foot, a shining length of intestine.

Their mouths are completely smeared with red.

We don't try to find Elmwood.

As far as we know, it sits right on the prairie and probably isn't safe anymore, if it ever was. So we go to the only place we know, the only place that could possibly hold a future for us.

We go home.

The journey is much shorter than the one we took to get here, but the lack of supplies makes it twice as difficult to survive. We all do, but by the time we make it to the foot of the mountain, our clothes are much bigger on us than before, and we can hardly walk on our own.

But we do. We abandon the wagon, and the children ride on Blackjack as Emily and I lead him up, up, up the path that goes to the clouds, to our cabin, to our home. We gorge on wild strawberries and water from the creeks. We refuse to give up. And when our cabin finally comes into view, just as tiny as when we left it but now with more than enough space to hold our entire family, we all burst into tears.

The air is frigid, and the first flakes of winter begin to fall as we huddle together inside the empty cabin. I tell the children that tomorrow we will make the last stretch, to the settlement on the other side of the mountain, and then all of this will finally be over. They shiver as they fall asleep.

I wonder if Henry will be there tomorrow. I wonder if he'll ask about our baby. I wonder if I'll be able to resist killing him for suggesting the prairie to my pa. Emily's breathing becomes rhythmic, and my eyelids flutter down, heavy and sleepy. I yawn.

But then there is a sound that makes me snap more awake than I've ever been in my life. Something outside the cabin, growing louder as it approaches, and my heart feels as though it may collapse.

It is the sound of Pa's fiddle, warped and thin and

drastically out of tune, somewhere out there in the dark woods.

Emily and the children sleep as soundly as ever.

The fiddle is playing "Come, Holy Ghost."

* * * * *

ACKNOWLEDGMENTS

The gratitude I feel for those who have supported me in my dream of becoming a published author is limitless:

Joanna Volpe, my incomparable literary agent who stuck by my side, tirelessly, for over four years before I finally got my foot in the door with a book deal. JoJo Baggins, words cannot describe how grateful I am for your patience and never-ending encouragement. I won't forget about that surprise bacon pizza feast for as long as I live! Besides being an excellent business-woman, you are also one of the kindest, most thoughtful people I've ever met. I'm proud to be able to call myself your client and your friend.

TS Ferguson, my kick-ass editor, as well as my incredible team at Harlequin Teen—in marketing, Mary Sheldon, Melissa Anthony and Amy Jones. In publicity, Jennifer Abbots. The awesome design team that created my creepy cover, Kathleen Oudit, Tara Scarcello, and Bora Tekoqul. Second-reads wizard Natashya Wilson. And to TS again: thank you for loving horror as much as you do. The first time we spoke on the phone I knew that you were someone I'd be insanely lucky to work with. I look so forward to whatever comes next for us as a spook-tacular duo!

Roxie Blackwood, longtime reader of everything I've ever written (including my Harry Potter fan fiction in high school) and fairy godmother extraordinaire. I am so lucky to have you in my life, sister-friend! Love you forever.

Kody Keplinger, the very first writer friend I ever made online and someone who has never stopped believing in me from the time she read the first chapter of my first book. I can't thank you enough for everything you've done to help me throughout this crazy experience, my dear!

My girls over at YA Highway: thank you for your friendships, wisdom, and awesome company at writing retreats over the years: Steph, Kir, KFH, K Botts 5000, V. Roth, Kris, Sumy, Sarah, Leila, Lee Bross the Baus, Kaits, Deb, and Emilia. You all rock my socks. Meese love forever!

Early reader Dawn Kurtagich, for her enthusiasm and kindness no matter what.

Everybody at New Leaf, but especially Danielle Barthel and Jaida Temperly, aka the best agency assistants *ever*!

Stephen King and R. L. Stine, for writing stories that made me fall head-over-heels in love with horror.